TRAPPED IN THE SECRET PASSAGE

The Castle Mystery Series

Dieter B. Kabus

Here's Life Publishers
P.O. Box 1576, San Bernardino, CA 92402

The Castle Mystery Series
TRAPPED IN THE SECRET PASSAGE
by Dieter B. Kabus

Cover Illustration by Peter Pohle

Published by
HERE'S LIFE PUBLISHERS, INC.
P.O. Box 1576
San Bernardino, CA 92402

HLP Product No. 951095
Printed in the United States of America.

Library of Congress Cataloging-in-Publication Data

Kabus, Dieter, 1941-
    Trapped in the secret passage.
    (The Castle mystery series)
    Translation of: Die Fünf Geschwister lösen das Geheimnis
der Abenteuerburg.
    Summary: Back at the castle for another vacation, five
brothers and sisters rely on God's help and protection to
solve a mystery involving ancestral paintings, a dishonest art
student, long-forgotten escape routes, and a secret room that
does not appear on any blueprint.
    [1. Castles—Fiction. 2. Mystery and detective stories.
3. Christian life—Fiction. 4. Brothers and sisters—Fiction]
I. Title. II. Series: Kabus, Dieter, 1941-   . Castle mystery series.
    PZ7.K115Tr 1986 [Fic] 85-27316
    ISBN 0-89840-125-9 (pbk.)
Translated from the German
    Original Title: Die Fünf Geschwister Lösen Das Geheimnis
Der Abenteuerburg
    © 1981, Verlag Schulte + Gerth Asslar

FOR MORE INFORMATION, WRITE:

L.I.F.E. —P.O. Box A399, Sydney South 2000, Australia
Campus Crusade for Christ of Canada —Box 300, Vancouver, B.C., V6C 2X3, Canada
Campus Crusade for Christ —103 Friar Street, Reading RGI IEP, Berkshire, England
Lay Institute for Evangelism —P.O. Box 8786, Auckland 3, New Zealand
Great Commission Movement of Nigeria —P.O. Box 500, Jos, Plateau State Nigeria, West Africa
Life Ministry —P.O. Box Bus 91015, Auckland Park 2006, Republic of South Africa
Campus Crusade for Christ International—Arrowhead Springs, San Bernardino, CA 92414, U.S.A.

CONTENTS

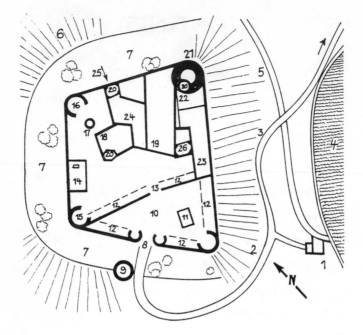

GROUND PLAN OF THE CASTLE:

1. Old Mill
2. Steep slope
3. Road to the village
4. Lake
5. Brook with waterfalls
6. The castle hill
7. Deep moat
8. Drawbridge
9. Outer tower
10. Entranceway
11. Apartment
12. Former farm buildings
13. Entrance to inner castle
14. Chapel
15. Western tower
16. Northern tower
17. Well
18. Residence
19. Knights' Hall
20. Stairway
21. High tower
22. Living room of castle
23. Outbuilding
24. Main building
25. Double wall
26. Stairway

Return to the Castle

"Wake up!" Fifteen-year-old Anne shook her younger sisters Katie and Rebecca until they were awake. Their brothers, Paul and Eric, put their books aside and looked out of the window of the train.

Katie, eleven years old, yawned. "Why did you wake us up so soon?"

Anne tapped her wristwatch with her finger. "In ten minutes we should be there!"

"What? We've slept that long?" Rebecca rubbed her eyes.

Anne nodded. "You've slept for more than two hours!"

"Seems like only ten minutes to me," Rebecca muttered.

"Eric!" warned Anne. Her ten-year-old brother was trying to shove a piece of paper underneath the train seat with his foot.

He sighed and bent down to pick it up. *Having four older brothers and sisters sure isn't easy!* he thought.

After they repacked their travel bags and lifted their suitcases down from the overhead rack, the children sat back and looked expectantly out the window. Their Great Dane, Tawny, lay obediently on the floor, observing everything with watchful eyes.

A few months earlier the Baker family had come to Germany so Mr. and Mrs. Baker could work with Outreach to Youth. They had spent their first weeks vacationing at a castle owned by Baron von Zerbach. There they had solved the mystery of *The Secret Treasure*. As a reward, the baron had promised the Bakers they could return to stay at the castle any time.

Now, during their school break, the children finally had a chance to come back.

"We can't go with you," their father had said. "But we know we can trust you to take care of one another. But just in case," he added with a smile, "I'm putting Anne in charge, because she's the oldest."

The train whistled as it carried them to the village near the castle.

Eric squirmed restlessly in his seat. "I can't wait to get back to the castle!" he exclaimed.

"I wonder if we'll have another adventure," Katie said, her eyes shining with anticipation.

Something's Wrong Here!

The next morning Katie was the first one to the kitchen of their apartment in Baron von Zerbach's castle. Singing happily, she set the table. The smell of toast soon brought the two boys to the kitchen.

"We came just in time to dig right in!" Paul exclaimed.

"Not so fast!" answered Katie. "The eggs aren't ready."

Eric went to the window that overlooked the inner courtyard. As he stood looking out, he heard the sound of a car. He watched as a station wagon entered the yard and stopped at the palace, the main building of the castle. A young man, blonde and bearded, got out. He wore a brown beret. His jeans and T-shirt looked worn. Paul came over to the window to stand beside his younger brother. They watched as the man, who looked to be about 25 years old, opened the back of the station wagon.

"That must be Mr. Grabinsky, the baron's nephew, the artist the Martins told us about," Paul said.

"Man, he's really been shopping!" exclaimed Eric. "That's enough food for a whole month."

"Maybe he's just shy and doesn't want to go to town every day to meet people," Paul suggested. "You know how the Martins talked about his art. Maybe he's just heard too many of those remarks."

"Good morning," called Rebecca from the doorway. "You certainly did a good job of setting the table. Keep that up, and you'll be a good housekeeper some day."

"I suppose you're looking for one," Paul said. "If I weren't your brother, I'd probably have a chance of getting the job. Only I didn't set the table. Katie did."

"Too bad! I guess she gets the credit," replied Rebecca with a smile.

The children said grace and ate breakfast. Paul, buttering his fifth slice of toast, asked, "Well, what do we do today?"

"Explore the castle!" responded Eric.

"Yes, I'd love to see the secret cellar where we found the treasure," Anne said.

"Okay, who's in favor of exploring the castle?" asked Paul.

Everyone's hand shot up.

After clearing the table and washing the dishes, the five Bakers hurried eagerly to the entrance of the main building.

Katie unlocked the door, then whispered, "First to the Knights' Hall?"

"Why are you whispering?" Paul asked. "We were given the key so we could see the castle. So what if someone sees us?"

"Sure," answered Katie, "but who knows that?"

The children entered the Knights' Hall. Eric touched the panel, and the secret door flew open.

The long, dark passage lay ahead.

"We forgot our flashlight!" Eric exclaimed.

"Be a good kid and get it," Katie said. "It's hanging in the closet in the hall."

Paul walked up to one of the suits of armor. "Remember when I was in one of these? I thought I was going to have a heart attack, but Professor Crippen didn't discover me."

"I wonder how things would have turned out if he had," Anne mused.

"What are you up to?" Katie looked over at Rebecca.

"Do you smell something?" Rebecca asked, sniffing the air.

"There is something strange. Maybe it's coming from the hall," suggested Anne.

"No! It's an oily smell," Rebecca said.

"Oily?" Anne asked.

"Yes, from this direction." Rebecca pointed to the back part of the Knights' Hall. "The smell is much stronger there."

The four children sniffed their way around the room.

Suddenly Rebecca cried out, "I know! It's the paintings!"

"The paintings?" Paul asked, looking up at the pictures on the wall.

"Sure! Come here and see for yourself!"

"Weird!" Paul exclaimed. "Maybe these old paintings have been touched up," he suggested, taking a closer look. "Sure looks like it. Check this," he said with growing excitement. "On the first eight pictures the surface is smooth. On the last two there are lots of cracks!"

Eric returned with the flashlight and joined the

11

others, who were examining the paintings hung around the hall.

"Something's wrong here!" Paul said. "The paintings show the lords of the castle, who have lived here over a period of four hundred years. On the small bronze plaques you can see their dates. This first painting shows Dieterich, 1483 to 1526."

"1483. The year Martin Luther was born," Anne said.

"This was also the nobleman who hid the treasure and who was later killed by the leader of the Peasants' Revolt," added Eric.

"Right!" answered Paul. "But I've noticed something else. The next painting reads: 'Guntar, 1504 to 1546.' Could be a son. And here, 'Neithard, 1525 to 1589. Archibald, 1550 to 1605. Hansjorg, 1573 to 1604. Wolfram, 1603 to 1636. Theoderic, 1625 to 1675. Siegfried, 1648 to 1702.' But now—look! The ninth painting shows 'Gotthard, 1723 to 1801,' and the tenth, 'Waltar, 1750 to 1833.' There are two generations missing."

"Maybe those lords were never painted," Anne suggested.

"Could be, but I don't think so," Paul replied.

"Why not?" asked Eric.

"Look at the white wall near the first painting."

Rebecca walked over to the spot and called out, "Sure enough. Paul was right. There was a picture hanging here. Part of the wall, as big as a painting, is a lighter color than the rest. You can even see the nail where the painting was hung."

"And now check the wall beyond the last painting," Paul said triumphantly.

"You're right!" exclaimed Rebecca. "Again the lighter spot. That means two of the twelve paintings are missing."

"And, so no one would discover it, all the paintings were hung one beside the other," declared Katie. "But why would two be missing?"

A puzzled silence followed.

"Well, we could ask somebody," Eric suggested.

"Who?" asked Paul.

"Baron von Zerbach's nephew—or Frau Martin."

"Sure, why not?" Katie agreed. "First we'll ask the nephew. He's an art student and would probably know."

"But before that I'd like to finish seeing the castle again," begged Anne.

"Okay," replied Eric. "We'll see the castle first!"

Katie entered the secret passageway, which led to the cellar where they had found the treasure a year ago. "Eric, please hand me the flashlight," she requested.

"No—I went back for it, so I get to lead the way!"

With hearts pounding, the children descended the steep stairs. The musty air took their breath away. Falling drops of water up ahead broke the stillness. Slowly the children advanced. At the spot where the treasure had been found, they stopped. The opening in the wall was sealed up again.

"To think we found Professor Crippen here and were able to save him at the last minute," said Rebecca, as if to herself.

"I'm cold! Let's go back," suggested Anne.

Silently the children found their way back. When they reached the staircase, Paul called out, "Whoever reaches the tower first is the winner!"

They all raced up the stairs, taking two and three steps at a time, and ran along the hall leading to the tower. They hurried up the narrow winding staircase to the upper platform, which was covered with a stone roof.

"Whew! I'm dizzy!" complained Rebecca, out of breath.

"What a beautiful view!" Anne looked out on the scene stretching below.

"The old mill with the waterwheel is still there," observed Eric. "I wonder if we can visit it this year?"

"You'd have to find out who owns it," answered Anne. "We could ask Frau Martin. Maybe she'd know."

"I'm tired!" Katie said. "Besides, what's for lunch?"

Anne shrugged her shoulders. "We have to plan our meals and go shopping. Today we'd better just use one of the cans Mom sent along."

The children left the platform and descended the winding stairs. Rebecca stopped to examine one of the openings through which a gun could be fired and which now gave some light to the staircase. Suddenly she stopped. *Were those voices she was hearing? No—it must be a mistake.* But as she continued, she again heard noises. Parts of words spoken by men's voices drifted upward from somewhere. She pressed her ear against the gun opening and listened intently. The voices seemed to be coming from one of the buildings below. *Maybe in the floor below, there's another opening,* she thought, her mind racing. *I have to find out!*

Quickly she skipped down the stairs. A flight down she found another opening. Carefully she leaned forward and listened. She could hear the voices a little more clearly, but she could not hear enough to make any sense of the words. *If only I could see,* she thought. The gun holes gave her a limited view of the landscape, but she needed to see the buildings below from which the voices came.

Meanwhile, the others discovered that Rebecca was missing. They all began to call her name.

Rebecca felt an angry flush of blood rise to her face. *They would have to yell*, she thought with dismay. Disappointed that she hadn't been able to discover more, she went down to join the others.

"Oh, there you are! Didn't you hear us?" asked Anne.

"Of course, I heard you!" Rebecca muttered. "You were yelling loud enough!"

Anne shook her head, not understanding her sister's reaction. "Come on, we have to go."

Something's wrong, thought Anne. *I know Rebecca. Maybe she's discovered something and is keeping it a secret. Well, I guess we'll find out eventually.*

Rebecca's brain continued its feverish pace. *There had been at least two voices. That meant that there were at least two men talking together. If only I could hear the art student's voice, then I'd know whether there are two or three people here.*

"Wait a minute! I'd like to know something about the two missing portraits. Are you coming with me?" Paul said.

"Sure, we're coming!" Katie replied.

"Stop!" To show the importance of what he was about to say, Eric raised his hand for quiet. "We'd better be careful!"

"Careful! Why?" Anne's raised eyebrows showed her surprise.

"Well, just suppose there is something crooked about this. It could be dangerous for us!"

"Maybe there's an international crime syndicate at work here," whispered Paul mysteriously.

"Oh, stop being childish!" Anne groaned.

"I want to say something," said Rebecca, looking

serious. "Maybe Eric is right, and you're making fun of him!"

"All right," agreed Anne. "Let's hear some suggestions before we go ahead."

Katie was the first to come up with an idea. "Eric can wait for us at our apartment. If we're not there at a certain time, he could call Inspector Martin."

"That's a good idea," said Anne. "It's now 11:45. By 11:55 one of us must be back with you, Eric. Get it? *Must be!* And by noon we must *all* be back."

"Wait a minute," said Katie thoughtfully. "Eric, if you see a man coming back with us, don't open the door. Just call Inspector Martin immediately."

"Oh, wow," he sighed. "How exciting! I'm the one who has to go back to the house." Eric took the key and quickly went down the stairs.

"What do we ask Herr Grabinsky?" Katie looked at Paul.

"We could tell him that we noticed the pictures in the Knights' Hall were being restored," Paul answered.

"You always come up with the right words!" Katie said.

"We could also say that we noticed two pictures were missing and that we think they are probably being redone just now," Paul added. "We could ask him to show us how it's done."

The children all agreed to this, then went over to the art student's quarters. Katie lifted the door knocker. Before she let go, she looked around at the others with a knowing look. For a moment, all the children thought back to the time a few months ago. Then another door knocker had been the key to the big secret!

Katie released the door knocker, and it re-sounded with a loud thud. The door opened.

16

"Hello, Herr Grabinsky," Paul began. He introduced himself and the others. Then he told about their discovery.

The young art student listened, his face almost without expression. "Yes, well," he started out, "actually, I'm not too thrilled with your discovery. It was to have been a surprise for my uncle, Baron von Zerbach. He turns fifty this year, so the restoration of the paintings was to be a gift to him. The paintings of our ancestors are old—some already several hundred years old. The paint was peeling. The restoration is very costly, so my uncle kept putting it off. Now I have two friends who are specialists in this field." The young man rocked back and forth on his feet, paused, then continued. "Yes, they just received the pictures and are restoring them—at a price only a friend would charge, you see."

"How long does it take to do one painting?" asked Katie.

"Oh, about a week. Soon I will be able to pick up the two."

The children thanked him and turned to leave.

The young man stood at the door to watch them go. He stared after them in anger, and in his pockets his hands balled into tight fists. He turned, locked the door carefully, went to the phone, and dialed.

Following the Trail

When the children neared their apartment, they saw Markus and Andreas Martin in the yard. The Martins lived in the village, where their father was a police officer. The Baker children had become good friends with the Martins during their first adventure at the castle.

"Hello," the Martin boys called.

"Hey, good to see you," Paul said. "We planned to visit you tomorrow, but something happened. Now we'll come the day after tomorrow. Okay?"

"Sounds good," Markus replied.

"We just spoke to Herr Grabinsky," Katie reported.

"What did you think of him?" Andreas asked.

"He's too skinny!" Katie replied.

"He's too what?"

"He's too skinny!"

Puzzled, Andreas looked at the others. "Yes, he's thin. But why too skinny?"

"He bought all those groceries. He ought to be fatter."

"What, he was shopping today again?" Andreas asked. "I saw him buying lots of groceries just a week ago. When I told my story over lunch, Markus said he'd seen Grabinsky buying lots of stuff the week before."

Rebecca could hardly keep quiet. She would have loved to tell about the voices she had heard.

"Well, we must go now," Markus said. "See you the day after tomorrow!" The two Martin boys headed toward the castle gate.

"Come on into the apartment," Rebecca said to her brothers and sisters. "I have something important to tell you."

I knew it! thought Anne.

As soon as they were seated in the living room, Rebecca told them about the voices she had heard.

"That's why he needs so many groceries!" Katie exclaimed.

Thoughtfully, Eric began, "Maybe he has visitors..."

"...who have to hide," interrupted Anne.

"What do you mean, *hide*? He doesn't have to introduce his friends to the whole neighborhood!" Paul exclaimed.

"We'll find out!" Katie said.

"How?"

"Listen," said Katie. "We should invite him for supper tonight and ask him to tell us about his art work. We'll listen very carefully, and maybe we'll find out whether there are others in the castle with him."

"Good idea," agreed Paul. "Let's go right back to him now."

Grabinsky opened the door. His eyes narrowed with suspicion. "You're back? What is it you want this time?" He sounded annoyed.

Katie, upset by the look on the young artist's face, spoke hesitantly. "Herr Grabinsky, we decided that since you are here alone, you must be very lonesome. We came to invite you over for supper. If you want to, you could tell us something about modern art."

The student's face lit up briefly. "I'm not alone—well, I mean, I don't feel alone or lonely. I need to get lots of rest in order to do my work here. I rather enjoy seeing no one for days. When I need company, I'll let you know. Thanks anyway." He gave them a forced smile, stepped back into the room, and locked the door.

Silently the children returned to their apartment.

"So, it's true," Anne said. "He is hiding someone."

Eric agreed. "We have to find out who it is. Maybe we should go back to the tower."

The five children left the house, entered the palace, and headed toward the tower staircase. They stopped at the small gun hole where Rebecca had first heard the voices.

Eric climbed to the edge of the opening. "Too bad! I can't see a thing. But I've got an idea." Quickly he withdrew from the narrow opening. "We can look down on the castle from the tower platform."

The children hurried up the winding stairs. Paul made it up first. He leaned far across the railing and looked down. Anne arrived next, and with a cry of alarm she grabbed Paul's legs.

"Are you crazy?" she yelled.

"No!" he answered. "I'm not going to fall!"

Soon all of them were leaning out and looking down at the castle grounds.

"The voices came from the left," Rebecca recalled. "They must have been coming from the building over there," she said, pointing across the courtyard.

"Do you realize which building that is?" Katie asked.

"What do you mean?"

"Don't you understand? I bet that's the room with the mysterious windows!" Katie exclaimed.

A year ago the children had discovered the windows, but the baron had told them that no one knew which room they belonged to. According to him, no one had ever entered the room, because the entrance to the room had never been discovered. The children clambered down off the railing and looked at each other.

"We have to find out what's going on there, no matter what the cost!" Katie said.

"Well," laughed Anne, "we'll have to talk about the price we're willing to pay after we figure out how to investigate that building."

Eric looked down to the yard below. "If it weren't so far down, one of us could be let down over the wall to look."

Paul's face lit up. "Let's lower something down!"

The others looked at him questioningly.

"A microphone, for example, so we could listen in on the conversation," Paul suggested. "We do have one that came with our tape recorder." He looked down over the railing. "I don't know how much loss of power there would be with about a hundred feet of cord. If we use the gun hole, we won't need such a long cord."

"But Rebecca heard words she couldn't understand," Eric said. "You won't hear anything more with a tape recorder."

"But if we lower a mike with a long pole, it could work," Paul replied.

"That's crazy, but let's do it!" Katie said moving toward the stairs.

"Wait a minute!" Paul shouted. "First we need to make a mental picture of the exact direction and the distance."

"The pole will have to be a least twenty feet long," Rebecca said.

"A bean pole," suggested Anne.

"It would be too long to get it up the winding staircase," Katie said.

"We could cut it in two and tie the pieces together again at the gun hole," Anne said.

"Well—that might work," Paul said doubtfully.

"Better to have something we could fit together —like a fishing rod," Eric suggested.

Katie gave her younger brother a quick pat on the shoulder. "Wow! That's it! There should be a shop in the village where we could pick up a fishing rod."

"Sure, let's go!" Katie agreed.

"Wait a minute! Besides that, we'll need another thirty feet of cord for the microphone," Paul added. "And a cheap microphone with a round head would be a good idea too. Our mike wouldn't pick up sounds all around it as well as from far away like a round one would."

The Bakers left the tower and walked to the village. The girls looked for a sporting goods store; the boys, for a shop with electronic equipment. Both soon found what they were looking for.

The girls chose the longest fishing rod they could find.

"Well, with such a fishing rod and your talent,

our lake will soon be empty of fish," teased the young clerk.

"You'll laugh," Rebecca said, "but we don't want to catch fish with it."

"No fish? Why then are you buying a rod?"

"We do want to catch something. But not fish, only voices," Rebecca explained.

"Voices?"

"Yes, voices."

"Are you here for a visit?" the clerk inquired. "Then you must be at the castle."

"How did you know that?" Katie asked.

The clerk laughed. "If you were here visiting relatives, I'd have seen you before. There aren't any other tourists here. The only vacation place is at the castle."

"Good thinking!" commented Anne.

Pleased by her compliment, the young man continued, "Last year someone found a treasure there."

A voice called from the back of the store.

"Sorry, I must go. Please pay the cashier. Goodbye!" The clerk hurried off.

As the girls were standing around outside, Anne exclaimed, "He was a neat guy!"

"Yes, he was," Katie said. "But I wish that Rebecca hadn't said what she did."

"Fishing for voices. No one could guess anything from that," Rebecca replied defensively.

Meanwhile the boys had found the electronics shop. A woman led them over to a counter. "I hope you can find what you need here," she said.

Paul inspected the various extension cords and electrical wiring. "There are plenty of cords here, but they're all too short," he said to the clerk. "We need a thirty-foot length."

"My husband and his assistant are out just now

24

putting up a TV antenna. In two or three hours they should be back. You'll have to return then. There is enough wiring here and plenty of plug-ins, but I can't solder the wires for you."

"Oh, I can do that! It takes only a few minutes," said Paul confidently.

"Really? The cord has many tiny wires," replied the woman.

"No, only two," Paul said.

Paul went back to the counter to look for a three-pronged plug. He inspected the various wires, picked one up, and said, "This is just what we need. All I need now is a soldering iron. In a few minutes it will be all done."

The woman looked at the cord and said, "I see only one wire, and your plug has three prongs."

"The center one is the ground; the other two are bridged over and connected to the wires," Paul said.

"Are you sure?" The woman looked at him questioningly.

"Yes. May I show you?"

The woman led the boys to a workroom. "To the left are the soldering irons."

In minutes Paul had succeeded in attaching the pronged end and the plug-in to either end of the cord and had tried it on the tape recorder.

"I didn't think you could do it," said the woman when she saw how well everything was working. "My husband will be surprised when I tell him about this."

She told the boys how much the wiring cost, and Eric took the money from his pocket to pay. Together with the change, the woman gave them two extra coins. "Here, get yourself some ice cream!"

The boys thanked her and left the shop.

Fishing for Voices

During lunch Paul and Eric fidgeted restlessly. Both were thinking about their plans for the afternoon and wondering what information the recording might give them.

Suddenly Rebecca broke into their thoughts. "We forgot something!" she exclaimed.

The others waited for her to continue.

"We plan to hold the microphone near the window, because we think that behind it is a room in which some unknown people are staying."

"We all know that!" cried Anne impatiently. "What did we forget?"

With a hurt look Rebecca continued. "You'd already know, if you hadn't interrupted me! We can't see the window, and our microphone might hang right in front of it and be discovered."

"You're right," replied Anne humbly. "We never thought of that!"

Quietly the children nibbled away at their lunch, lost in thought.

"The best view we have is from the tower

27

platform," said Eric, as if to himself.

"Can't we do both?" suggested Katie. "We could put the microphone on the fishing rod and shove it through the gun hole, and at the same time guide the mike with a fishing line."

Paul spoke up. "That's a good idea, but better yet, we need another fishing rod on the platform to guide and control the first one."

"Right! We'll buy another one," decided Rebecca. "Then we can also go fishing by twos later on. How about it? You boys run back to the shop, while we do the dishes and clean up here."

The boys nodded, and soon they were on their way. In less than an hour they were back with another fishing rod.

The children started out and made it into the tower without being seen. Quickly they got out one of the fishing rods. Paul attached the microphone to one end of it and switched on the tape recorder. It worked! The needle indicated that sound was being recorded.

The children separated. Anne and Katie went to the platform to work the second rod. Rebecca planned to attach the fishing hook to the end of the rod, then push it over the edge and hang on. Paul was to monitor the recording. Eric was to be the runner. The thought of hurrying up and down the spiral stairs to maintain contact between the two groups didn't exactly thrill him, but he recognized the importance of the job, so he agreed to do it.

Filled with anticipation, Rebecca and Paul watched their fishing rod. Suddenly it was lifted at the tip. Carefully, with a pounding heart, Rebecca moved the rod farther out through the gun hole. Now the adventure could begin!

"We could never have managed alone from

here." Rebecca turned toward Paul, who had put on the earphones and was listening intently.

Paul turned to Eric and whispered, "Go tell the girls not to let the mike hang so close to the wall. The wind is knocking it against the brick."

Eric nodded and ran off.

Meanwhile Anne and Katie had wound up the reel as far as possible. Anne was holding the rod, while Katie was looking out over the castle grounds. Eric appeared on the platform, and Katie asked, "Well, did they hear anything yet?"

Eric nodded and explained why he had come. Carefully Katie leaned over and pushed the fishing rod farther out.

"Any message?" Eric asked.

The two girls shook their heads.

"Okay, I'll run down again."

Paul was still listening closely. The conversation, between two men, had turned to sports. Both men seemed very well-informed, quoting names, scores, and times of games. He gave a worried look at the spinning tape and turned to Rebecca. "Do you want the headphones for a while?"

Rebecca shrugged her shoulders. "We can listen to the tape tonight."

Paul looked over at Eric. "You want them?"

"Sure!" Eric took the earphones, put them on, and sat down in the narrow opening.

Paul climbed the tower stairs.

"Hey, tell us!" cried Katie. "What did you hear?"

"A sports' report, three hours long!" Paul replied.

"Nothing else?"

Paul shook his head.

"Do you think those men are hiding?" Anne asked.

"It looks that way," Paul said.

"If you're right, I don't understand why Herr Grabinsky is so careless," Anne observed. "It does look funny when someone who is supposed to be living alone buys so much food."

The three children sat quietly, lost in thought.

Katie yawned. "The time here passes as slow as it does at school!"

"Depends on the subject!" Anne muttered.

Paul stood up. "I'm going back down. Maybe Eric has something interesting to report."

When Paul appeared at the gun hole, Eric removed the earphones. "Everything is pretty quiet. I can't hear much."

"What could they be doing?" asked Rebecca, giving Eric a puzzled look.

He shrugged his shoulders. "They seem to be working at something, because sometimes I hear a soft scratching noise."

"A scratching noise?" Paul said. "Hand me those earphones, please." After a few minutes Paul took them off again. "Total silence!" he murmured.

When the tape recorder clicked off, eveyone relaxed.

"Enough!" Paul pulled in the fishing rod carefully, undid the hook, and signaled the girls above with three short tugs at the line. After everything was packed up, the children started home.

Back in the apartment they flopped into chairs to rest.

Suddenly, Rebecca jumped up. "Come on!" she said. "Let's use this time to listen to the tape."

"We don't need to listen to side one. I heard every word," Paul said.

"I'd still like to hear it," declared Rebecca, and started the tape.

"Okay, go ahead!" Paul snapped. "I'm going to the bedroom to read. I'll be back in an hour."

The remaining four children listened carefully to the conversation on the tape but didn't hear anything unusual. Then, after about a half hour, Anne looked up, startled. "Could I hear that sentence again?"

The others nodded, looking at each other.

Anne rewound the tape, turned the volume up, and pushed the play button. All the children listened intently.

"There! Those are the words I want!" Anne rewound the tape once more and started it up again. Amid the scratchy noises a man's voice was saying, "Where's the blue paint? Oh, here."

"Did you hear that?" whispered Anne.

After they had listened to the same sentence several times, they shut the recorder off.

"They seem to be using paint," Eric said.

"I think so. But why are they hiding? Could they be restoring the paintings?" Anne asked.

"Maybe." Eric replied. "We have to find out. But how? We haven't located the secret passage that leads to the room they're in."

Just then Paul came back and asked, "Well, did you hear anything special?"

"We sure did!" Anne said, turning on the recorder.

Paul listened in astonishment. "I didn't hear that," he mumbled. "I'm sorry! It's a good thing you insisted on listening to it. What do we do now?"

"We must find out who these men are and what their plans are," Anne declared.

More Surprises!

The children slept late the next morning. Eric was the first to awaken. He leaped out of bed, took a shower, and got dressed. Ideas whirled through his head. He sat down in the living room, picked up a sheet of paper and a pencil, and tried to make a diagram of all the buildings on the castle grounds.

Suddenly he jumped up, left the house, and headed for the main building to climb the tower. If there is another secret passage, he reasoned, its exit must be somewhere outside the castle, in a place where it has never been discovered. It must have existed for several hundred years without being found. Baron von Zerbach had told the children that several families had used a secret passage to escape when the castle was surrounded during the Peasants' Revolt. Later, when they were captured, the families admitted there was a secret passage.

Eric climbed up to the platform and surveyed the surrounding mountainous countryside.

The foundation of the castle was laid on a huge

jutting rock. A wide moat separated the castle from the slope beyond. Eric studied the rocky slope. A secret passage would have had to run beneath the moat, because building it upward into the rocky wall would have taken years. Eric turned to study the valley below the castle. The wall of rock in this direction ended in a sheer drop. The passage could not possibly be there. Since the rock slope above, and the rocky drop below offered no possibility for a secret passage, it left only the areas to the sides of the castle. On one side the mountain road wound its way down to the village below. On the other side a brook flowed into the lake after passing by the old mill. They would have to investigate both sides carefully, Eric decided.

His survey completed, Eric started down the stairs. Suddenly he stopped short. What was that? He heard it clearly—a key turning in a lock! Then a door at ground level was opened. A man started up the flight of stairs. It was Grabinsky, the art student.

What should I do now? Eric wondered. *Just continue on my way? After all, I have every right to be exploring the castle.*

His curiosity got the better of him. Where was Grabinsky going? Moving softly, Eric left the stairway and hurried into one of the side halls from which doorways led to rooms, both to the right and to the left. Since the walls were thick, and the doorways were huge, Eric could easily hide in any one of them.

I hope he's not planning to come down this hall, thought Eric. Again he heard the footsteps on the stairs. A door opened and shut again. The sound of steps became more faint. *Where is he going?* Eric wondered.

Intent on finding the answer, Eric quietly went

back to the stairway, hurried up the stairs, carefully opened a door, and inched his way across the room to listen at a doorway at the end of it. He knew that beyond the door lay another spiral stairway—one not as wide or beautiful as the main one. Grabinsky was still going up. Should Eric open the door? He was afraid the door would creak loudly if he tried that, so he took his hand off the doorknob. Suddenly he heard a squeaky doorknob turn, then silence.

Eric waited a few minutes, his heart pounding. Then slowly he pushed the door. It swung open without a sound. Carefully he looked up the open stairwell. Nothing! *That could only have been the door to the attic*, he thought, *but what does Grabinsky want up there?* He decided to wait for Grabinsky to return.

The minutes ticked away, and nothing happened. Eric looked at his watch.

"A half hour!" he grumbled, and fell into deep thought. Suddenly he jumped up. He heard another doorknob squeak, and the sound of footsteps echoed from the walls of the stairway above. Eric ducked into the hallway, carefully closed the door, then went back to his hiding place, hoping not to be seen. When the sound of the footsteps came from below him, he crept over to peer through the wrought-iron railing that decorated the staircase. There was Grabinsky.

After the door below had been closed and all was quiet again, Eric stood, not sure what to do next. His curiosity and love of adventure were battling with his instinct to be careful.

His curiosity won. He slipped quietly up the stairs. Again his heart pounded as he stood before the door to the attic. The turn of the doorknob produced the same creaky sounds he had heard before. So this was the door Grabinsky had gone through!

Cautiously Eric opened the door and left it ajar to make sure he would hear any sounds coming from the stairs. He walked into the attic. Faint rays of light came in through cracks in the roof. He saw dusty furniture—a few chairs, a table, a cabinet, and several bookshelves. He went over to the window and was surprised to see that part of the dirty window had been wiped clean enough to look through. Had Grabinsky been watching someone from up there? But who? Eric turned to leave, carefully closed the door behind him, and went down. Finally he slipped across the yard and entered the apartment, where the others were at breakfast.

"Where were you?" Anne inquired.

"In the castle!"

"And?"

"I made a crazy discovery! Well, I'm not sure it's so crazy, but it's a discovery, all right."

"What? Tell us!" Katie cried.

Eric reached over for some toast. "Only after a third slice!"

"That's mean!" exclaimed Rebecca. But Eric began to talk as soon as he started buttering his toast.

"Crazy is right," agreed Anne. "So today we have to investigate the road leading to the castle and the brook running by the mill."

"There's something else. I saw Grabinsky!" Eric added.

"And?" Katie inquired. Four pairs of eyes watched him keenly.

"After the next slice!" Eric replied, enjoying the suspense.

36

Annoyed, Katie sprang to her feet. "You're acting dumb!"

"Okay, okay," Eric said and began to recount his discoveries.

"You could see the mill through the window? And the road?" Paul asked.

"No, only the short stretch leading to the mill."

"Grabinsky must have been watching someone," Anne suggested.

Eric shrugged his shoulders. "Maybe."

"Otherwise there were no windows, no door, or other exit?" Paul asked.

"No, I didn't see any."

"I think we should leave here at 9:30 and check out the road leading to the castle," Anne suggested.

The others agreed.

The search was harder than the children had imagined. At a distance of about thirty feet from each other, the children climbed the steep incline. Each carried a thick stick to poke into places that might look suspicious. In this way they covered a strip only 150 feet wide, so they went up and down two more times.

At two o'clock they sat down to lunch, a very tired bunch.

"Do we have to go investigate the other side today?" Rebecca asked as she filled her plate.

"We're all a bit tired," agreed Katie. "But if we should succeed..." She paused and looked at the others. "We could find the secret passage today."

"That would be great!" admitted Rebecca. "Let's go!"

The area was rocky, so the children found the descent difficult. Their second round brought them to the brook with its rapids. Their next round took them to the mill.* Surrounded by huge oaks, it stood near the shore of the lake. The children peered through the dirty windows and saw huge cogwheels amid the sturdy rafters. There were also millstones and other tools.

"It looks spooky in there!" Katie exclaimed. "But still I'd love to explore it."

The five Bakers went around the building. Suddenly Anne stopped.

"Look! The mill seems to be occupied." She pointed to faint tire tracks leading from the paved road to the wooden shack that had been added to the mill and seemed to be a garage.

"That's strange!" mumbled Paul, "Andreas and Markus would have told us if the mill was occupied."

"That was last year. Maybe things have changed since then," replied Katie.

"We could call Frau Martin and ask," suggested Rebecca.

"Come on," Katie urged. "Let's cover the rest of this territory. I'm getting tired."

Their search turned up no clues. Slowly the children climbed back up to the castle, thoroughly disappointed.

That evening they read from their devotional book and prayed together. Then the three girls went to bed. Paul wrote some postcards to his friends back home, and Eric called Frau Martin.

When he asked about the mill, she answered, "No, you cannot get into the mill. The owner died about a year ago. His only child, a daughter, lives abroad and hasn't been back here for a long time."

---

*See map: The brook (#5) flows past the old mill (#1). The children explored the steep slope (#2).

Eric thanked her and hung up.

"Well, what's the word?" asked Paul when Eric came back to the livingroom.

"The mill is not occupied, and the owner is far away."

"Weird!" murmured Paul and went back to writing his cards.

Still More Riddles

Over breakfast the Bakers discussed their puzzling discovery at the mill.

"Those tracks at the mill are not very old," Paul stated confidently. "Maybe two or three months."

"How do you know that?" Rebecca looked dubiously at her brother.

"If you didn't spend all your time playing with dolls, you'd know too!" Paul replied.

"I bow before your mature wisdom!" Rebecca quipped.

"If only we knew whether there are people using the mill," Eric said.

"That won't be easy to find out," Katie remarked. "We can't watch the mill all the time."

"I have an idea," Anne declared. "Yesterday, when I pushed the door latch, I noticed that the door opened outwards. We could push a small stick into the ground in front of the door. No one would notice it in the grass. Then if it's bent or broken, we would know somebody opened the door."

"We could do the same at the shack or garage, if

41

that door opens outward," Katie suggested.

"Doors of garages and storage places always open outward," declared Eric. "Otherwise too much space would be wasted."

"Right! Let's go," Katie exclaimed.

The children, together with their dog, Tawny, went into the yard. Laughing and yelling, they ran down the road to the mill. Just before they reached it, Eric stopped.

"Wait!" he cried. "The mill is within sight of the castle. If someone is watching us, we should be careful so he doesn't see what we came to do."

"Good idea," agreed Rebecca. "The front door is no problem, since it's on the other side, but the door to the garage can be seen."

The children paused to lay plans. They agreed to crowd together. Eric would be in the back. He would bend over and push the stick into the ground in front of the door.

They walked to the door of the mill and stopped casually in front of it. Eric quickly bent down and pushed a one-inch stick into the ground. It took only two seconds. Then the children walked on, chattering loudly, while Eric remained kneeling to tie the laces on his right shoe.

Behind the shack they stopped.

"If only we could look in!" Anne exclaimed.

The siding boards were close to each other, and there were no cracks. Katie stepped close to the wall and inspected a knothole with her fingers. The center part moved easily. When Anne saw this, she said, "If we could get it out, we could peek inside."

"It would be hard to pull out," Katie declared, looking at her broken fingernail. "But we could push it in."

Anne looked around, picked up a sharp stone,

and banged at the knot. After a few attempts it fell away. Anne put her eye to the knothole.

"A car!" she cried with surprise.

"Lift me up, please!" Eric cried. "Yes, it's a car! Too bad it's so dark in there. It's hard to see anything."

Paul had been checking the wall for other knot-holes.

"Here's another one," he called. "Where's the stone?"

Anne pointed to the ground, and Paul picked up the stone. On his second try the knot fell away.

"I can see a license plate," he called. "It's only a few feet away!"

"Can you read it?"

"RUB-PX—but I can't read the numbers."

Rebecca wrote the letters in the dusty ground. "RUB—have you any idea where that could be?"

Anne and Katie shook their heads.

"On the round part you should see the name of the area the car is from. Can you make it out?" Anne asked.

Paul looked again. "No, it's too dark. But that's okay. We'll ask the Martins. Now, what do we do about the open holes. Anyone inside the garage would spot them immediately."

Rebecca solved the problem. She picked up some soft mud, formed two balls, and pressed one into each hole.

"Good enough?" she asked.

"Sure, if they stay put," said Paul. "Come on, let's go."

When they reached a spot from which they could easily see the castle, Eric stopped, bent down to pick up a rock, and called out excitedly, "Look what I found!"

All the others huddled around him. Eric whispered, "Keep looking at my stone and act cool. I figured this would happen."

"What?" Katie asked.

"We're being watched!" Again he cautioned, "Just act natural."

Katie bent down and pretended to be interested in the stone. "Who's watching?"

"I don't know!"

"From where?" Paul asked.

"From the castle, from the attic window."

"How can you see so far?"

"I see two lenses of binoculars reflecting the sunlight."

"Let's trade places," suggested Paul. He took the stone and held it up to the light, but looked past the stone to the castle.

"You're right!" he muttered.

"What do we do now?" Rebecca asked, looking worried.

"We'll keep on looking for stones," Eric suggested.

"Look!" called Paul. "Look what I found!"

When the four were close to him he said quietly, "Have you all seen it now?"

The others nodded.

"We'll go down to the shore of the lake now, just as if we were out for a hike," Paul said.

They skipped stones on the water for some time before they set out on their way back to the castle.

Home again, Katie said, "Let's have lunch now. Later Andreas, Simon, and Markus are coming."

"I'll call them and ask them to find out where that license plate is from," Anne said.

After she put down the receiver, she reported, "Andreas will check into it."

44

While the children were eating, the sky clouded over. Then rain began to fall.

"Oh no!" grumbled Paul. "If it rains, we can't go out."

"We can just stay here, or explore some more in the castle," suggested Rebecca. Her face lit up. "How would it be if I bake a cake we can eat later for a snack?"

"Great idea!" Eric exclaimed.

When the doorbell rang, the Bakers welcomed the Martin brothers.

Andreas turned to Anne. "Why were you curious about the area for which the letters RUB stand?" He paused. "There is no such place!"

"What?" Katie exclaimed in amazement.

"But I saw it with my own eyes," Paul declared.

"Then it must be a phony license plate!" Eric exclaimed.

"I could be wrong," Paul said hesitantly, "but I don't think so."

"What *are* you talking about?" Markus asked.

Rebecca told them the whole story including the missing paintings and the explanation Herr Grabinsky had given.

Markus said, "A year or two ago the baron told me about the poor condition of those paintings. He mentioned that it would be very costly to have them restored. And he will soon be fifty. All that is true."

Andreas broke in. "Maybe Grabinsky just likes secrets and really is trying to surprise his uncle."

"How do you know that the car in the mill garage has any connection with the artist?" Simon asked.

Katie groaned. "I can tell you have a police officer for a father. We thought we were on the

45

track of crooks who were working on the paintings. But—maybe we aren't."

"What made you suspect the men?" Markus asked. "The paintings are being restored. Crooks do copy paintings. Have you reason to believe the paintings in the hall are copies of the originals?"

"Not really," Anne said.

"Wait!" Eric jumped up. "Every picture has two sides. We looked at only one!"

"What do you mean?" Markus asked.

"Eric is talking about the back of the paintings," Paul explained. "If the back is new, then we would know the front is also new. If they're old, then the..."

"Enough!" Simon stopped him. "We get the rest. But you're right, then we would know. Let's find out!"

"Wait!" Rebecca held up her hand. "As you know, we women often have intuitions!"

Simon cleared his throat loudly. "Women, she says! Well, speak!"

"If there should be something to this, and we're seen..." She paused. "I'm for playing it safe."

"And what does that mean?" Simon asked.

"That we distract any possible observer."

"How?"

"Well, for example, two or three of us could climb the tower and call to the others in the yard," Rebecca said. "Meanwhile two could sneak into the Knights' Hall and inspect the paintings."

"All right, if you think it's necessary," agreed Andreas. "I would like to inspect the paintings, together with Paul."

"I volunteer to stay down," Anne offered.

"So do I," said Markus and Simon together.

Rebecca turned to Katie and Eric. "Come on, we're going up!"

46

The three climbed the tower. Paul and Andreas waited until they heard them call. Quickly they dashed to the Knights' Hall and took down the first painting.

"Where do we put it?" Andreas asked.

"On the rug," answered Paul. "It can't fall if it's on the floor."

As soon as they looked at it closely, Andreas whispered excitedly, "The canvas is new!"

"Sure enough!" Paul stared at the back side of the painting. "No doubt at all. Let's look at the others."

Soon all ten paintings lay on the rug.

"What a difference!" commented Paul, as he looked at one of the originals. "Come, let's hang them up again."

After the fifth picture, Paul froze. "Psst!" He motioned to Andreas.

Both boys stopped to listen. Voices of men and women were coming in through the window.

"Quick!" Paul exclaimed.

Hurriedly they replaced the other paintings. In their haste they did not notice that they changed the order of the last two paintings. After finishing their work, they went quietly over to the window and peeked out through the curtains.

They looked at each other and laughed! The people they had heard were some hikers who had made their way over to the castle. Paul and Andreas signaled the other children in the yard.

Anne called up to those in the tower, "Come on, let's have that cake Rebecca baked!"

When the three came down, Paul and Andreas joined them. They all walked across the yard to the Baker apartment.

As they sat around the table enjoying the cake,

Andreas asked, "Should we tell our father?"

Anne looked at him with a horrified expression. "No! We still have to finish our investigation. Later we'll need your father to make some arrests."

"You want to pretend you're being a detective yourself!" teased Simon.

Anne blushed. "Maybe I do!"

After the cake had disappeared, Markus asked Paul, "How are your guitar lessons coming?"

"Well, I'm making some progress."

"Let's sing together!" Andreas suggested.

The children agreed. Singing songs of faith calmed their feelings. The songs reminded them that they had nothing to fear, because Jesus, their best friend, was with them.

After they had sung for two hours, Markus suggested that they pray together.

Anne looked around and asked, "What will we pray for? It will be easy to give thanks, because we had an exciting day. But what do we ask for?"

"Maybe that nothing bad will happen to us and that we do all right throughout our adventure," Rebecca suggested.

Katie looked at the others. "Shouldn't we be praying for these men? They should turn to God and become honest people."

For a moment everyone was silent.

Finally Andreas replied, "You're right."

"Do we have the courage to pray for the impossible?" Rebecca asked.

"We discussed that in our Bible class," said Anne. "I think we have the courage to pray, but do we really believe that God can do the impossible? Think of the story in Acts 12. When Peter was in prison, the church prayed for his freedom. He was freed and went back to knock at their door. They didn't believe it was really Peter. They had prayed for this, but they didn't really expect a miracle."

"I think that one should not tell God what or when," Andreas offered. "If it fits into God's plan, He will answer immediately. But many never experience this. Sometimes one has to wait. So we just leave it up to the Lord to bless these men, as well as to bless us. God will do things right!"

The children joined in prayer.

When Andreas, Markus and Simon said goodbye, Eric asked, "Are you coming back here tomorrow?"

"We can't come tomorrow," answered Simon. "We have a job to do."

"Oh, what?" Rebecca asked.

"In town there are some older couples, members of our church, who have gardens but aren't able to look after them on their own. So, that's our job."

"Great! You're doing a good deed as well as making some money," Anne said.

"No, we don't ask for any pay. So we probably won't see you for a while. On Saturday and Sunday we're going to visit some relatives. And on Monday at 3 P.M. we have youth classes at church. Will you come?"

"Sure!" Anne agreed for all of them.

"Okay, God bless!" Markus said.

"You too!" cried Anne.

"Those guys are neat!" Paul exclaimed.

Tricked!

During breakfast the next day, the doorbell rang. Katie opened the door. There stood Herr Grabinsky. He took a step forward to stand in the doorway before Katie could close the door.

"Yes?" she stammered.

"I have come to make you an offer," the art student announced.

"An offer?" Katie repeated. Her mind was racing.

"Didn't you want to know something about art?" he asked.

"Yes," said Katie hesitantly. "Just a minute. Please, be seated." She pointed to a chair near the center of the room.

"No, thanks. I sit all day, so I'm glad to have a chance to be on my feet. But where are the others?"

Katie called out, "Paul, Rebecca, Eric. Herr Grabinsky is here. Please come down!"

Upstairs the children hesitated, trying to decide what to do. Rebecca looked worried.

"With Tawny here, nothing can happen," Paul

reassured her. "In case of a problem you call the Martins."

Rebecca nodded.

"Come on," urged Anne. "Let's go down before he gets suspicious."

"Well, there you are!" Grabinsky said as the children filed into the room. "I came to make you an offer."

Just then Tawny entered the room.

"What a giant dog!" Grabinsky exclaimed and began backing up. A loud growl from Tawny caused him to back still farther into a corner.

Paul saw the man's fear and cautioned him, "Don't move! The dog has no collar. I can't control him!"

What a line! Eric thought to himself. *Our Tawny wouldn't hurt anyone.*

But the warning had worked. When Grabinsky moved back to the center of the room, he did it very slowly.

"You seem to be interested in art," he began again. "I think such an interest should be fostered. I must go out on business tomorrow, and on my way back I'm coming through the village. As you may know, there is an art gallery there, which I want to stop at because of my upcoming exams. If you meet me there, I could explain to you the different periods of art. Unfortunately, because of my schedule, this is the only time I can do it. Now, how about it?"

The children hesitated.

"What's wrong? You asked for it, and now you're not sure?" Grabinsky's voice was filled with irritation.

"Yes," Paul decided. "We'll come with you."

The others agreed.

"There are five of you. Will you all come?" Grabinsky inquired.

"I'll ask Rebecca," Anne said and stepped into the next room.

Rebecca shook her head and whispered, "Not me!"

Anne came back. "Rebecca doesn't want to go, but..."

Grabinsky interrupted her. "No, that won't do! I'd like all of you to come. If I'm your guide, you'll be with an expert. You don't have to put up with an ignorant museum guide."

What conceit! thought Anne. She went over to Rebecca and winked. "You'll come?"

Rebecca hesitated, then nodded.

"All right," said Grabinsky. "The bus leaves around 12:30 from here, so we'll meet at the museum about two o'clock. On the way back, you can ride with me. Till then, good-bye."

When Katie closed the door behind him, the five Bakers looked at each other, bewildered.

"He can't kidnap all five of us!" Eric said.

"No," said Paul. "I think he just wants us all to leave the house at once."

"Well, we'll spoil that for him!" exclaimed Katie.

"Wait a minute!" Paul lifted a warning hand. "Then we'll never find out what he was trying to do. We should accept his offer, but also watch the house."

"You want to hide Tawny somewhere and later on ask her what she saw?" asked Katie with a smile.

"Oh, come on! We'll call the Martins and ask them to help us. Andreas can watch the house. We'll leave Tawny here and open the doors to all the rooms. She'll keep out any intruders. We'll take Markus and Simon to town with us. Markus can

53

keep an eye on the museum, and Simon can follow us around."

"Good plan!" exclaimed Rebecca. She dialed the Martin's number.

Andreas answered, and Rebecca explained everything to him. He was eager to help. "You can count on us! I'll be there by eleven. My brothers will start out on their bikes by one."

When Rebecca hung up, she exclaimed, "We have some good friends there!"

*   *   *

It was 2:15 the next day when the art student finally drove up and parked in front of the museum.

"Sorry," he said, as he got out, "but just as I was about to leave the castle, the restored paintings arrived. We need only the last one now, and our gallery of ancestors will be just like new!"

Just like new is right, thought Eric.

The tour proved to be more interesting than the Bakers had expected. They learned about the different art periods in history and what distinguished one period from another.

One of the Baroque paintings had several tiny holes. Using them as his example, Grabinsky explained the process of restoration. "The paintings must first be cleaned. There are hundreds of years of accumulated dust on some of them. This is done with a special solvent. Then a new backing is put on, and the holes are filled in."

"A new backing?" Katie asked.

"Yes, a new backing, pasted on over the old one, which is usually cracked and broken. This gives the painting new life for several hundred years."

"So, that's how it's done," said Paul softly. *That explains the new backings on the paintings*, he thought to himself. *I guess we were wrong.*

After the tour, Grabinsky took the children back to their apartment. They thanked him and ran inside.

"Should we call the Martins?" Katie asked eagerly.

"Not yet," said Eric. "Andreas has been watching the house until now. He needs at least ten minutes to get back home."

They were still waiting when the phone rang. Rebecca jumped up to answer. After a short conversation she reported, "Andreas was bored to tears. Nothing happened!"

"When did Grabinsky leave the castle?" Anne asked.

"About 1:55," Rebecca replied.

"What?" Anne jumped up. "Then he must have come directly to the museum."

Rebecca nodded.

"And when did the carrier deliver the paintings?" Katie asked.

"He didn't!" Rebecca said.

"What?" asked Katie and Paul together.

"That's right!" answered Rebecca. "There was no delivery van. Like I said, nothing happened!"

"What a liar!" Anne cried.

"Just to make us believe that the paintings are being restored somewhere else, he invited us to go to the museum with him," Paul said. "But the trap didn't succeed, because we know the paintings are being restored in the castle."

A Secret Is Revealed

The Bakers were now convinced that the baron's nephew, Herr Grabinsky, was not doing anything illegal, so their interest turned to the secret passage they thought might exist in the castle. They felt sure that any such passage must begin on the main floor of the palace. They carefully looked over every room, tapped on all the wooden trimmings, pushed at ledges, and inspected each fireplace.

Paul climbed into one of the chimneys. He discovered a small niche, explored it, but found nothing extraordinary.

When he crawled out, Anne exclaimed, "Look at your hands!"

"If you'd have been climbing through the soot, your hands would look like this too," Paul replied. "I have to look at the fireplace in the kitchen. When I've searched them all, I'll go back home for a shower."

When Paul returned from the kitchen, Eric said, "Have a look at this stove. You're already covered with soot."

The three girls entered.

"Why would there be a stove in the hall?" asked Anne.

"Two rooms could be heated with the one stove," explained Rebecca. "I looked it over carefully. Behind the wall there are two tiled stoves, one in the corner of each of the two rooms. They were probably bedrooms, and the servants could tend the fires from the hall during the night."

Eric interrupted Rebecca. "Stop! Paul, please jiggle the door."

"Why?"

"I think the tiles moved."

Paul quickly withdrew his hands. "You want everything to fall apart?"

"Of course not." Eric bent over, grabbed the stove door, and tried to give it a good jolt.

"He's right!" exclaimed Rebecca. "The whole thing is easy to move."

"Look over here," Eric carefully pulled at the edge of the stove door and pointed to a wooden ledge surrounding the trimming around the fire opening. It was obvious that it could be moved a fraction of an inch off the wall.

"It can't be moved over to the right side," said Katie.

"If only we could see the ledge from the top," Rebecca suggested.

Paul stepped up against the open stove and commanded, "Come on, Rebecca, step up on my shoulders."

No sooner had Rebecca climbed up on his shoulders when she cried, "Just as I thought! To the right the ledge is snug against the wall. To the left it lifts away from the wall." Rebecca jumped down. "Is it a secret door?"

"Looks like it," Paul said.

"Wait a minute!" Eric put his finger to his lips and listened. "There's a soft clicking sound here. Maybe the locking mechanism is behind it. Paul, why don't you feel around in the stove, seeing you..."

"Okay, okay. I know," Paul replied. "I already look like a chimney sweep." He explored the inside wall, then asked that his shirt sleeves be rolled way up, so he could try even higher. "There's no point to this. I can't reach the upper part."

Carefully Eric inspected the dark opening. "I'm getting a flashlight!" he said.

Paul looked at his sooty arm. "We should have thought of that sooner."

Soon Eric returned. He knelt down, put his head through the opening, turned this way and that, then asked for the flashlight and shined the light on the inside wall. "There's nothing unusual here," he said, standing up again.

"No bolt or lever, or anything like that?" Paul asked.

"Above the door there is a thick pin, but it doesn't move. In the metal lining there are many rivets. In one corner, sticking out of the wall, there's a flat piece of iron with a hole in the middle."

"Where?" asked Rebecca. "About here?"

"Yes, I think so," Eric said. "That's the place where I heard the soft clicking," he explained. "But I can't get to it. We need a hook of some sort."

"A fireplace poker!" suggested Katie. "There's one in the Knights' Hall."

She hurried off to get it. Soon she was back and said, "Here, try it with this."

Carefully Eric explored the corner with the tip of the poker. "I've got the hook in the hole now." He looked around for some advice. "Now what?"

"Pull down on it," suggested Rebecca.

Eric shook his head. "Won't go."

"Then try to pull sideways," she said.

Rebecca pulled at the stove damper when suddenly the entire decorative grating moved forward. With a cry she let go of the door. Eric sprang up, his eyes sparkling. Slowly he pulled open a door, which opened with loud squeaks. Behind it was an empty space some six feet wide, divided into an upper and a lower compartment. The bottom part was the fireplace, which they'd seen before. Above that was a space, three feet high, deep, and wide. A few pieces of decaying wood lay in it.

Disappointed, Paul sighed. "It's only a storage place for firewood. The green, wet logs were stored there to dry them out."

"Wouldn't the wood have started burning?" Eric asked.

Paul shook his head. "See, the layer of clay between the two places is very thick."

Eric looked at the bolt again. "That door must have opened very easily back then," he said, pointing to the rusty spring. "The bolt would be helped open by the spring. In this hole there must have been a tiny chain that stretched across the pin and hung down near the opening. Anyone who needed to could open the door and never even get dirty fingers." Lost in thought, he began banging the walls around the storage area.

"Hey, what's that?" Katie cried, as Eric reached the right side. Curious, he again tapped both sides.

"The right side sounds hollow compared to the left," said Katie. "This fireplace heated both the tiled stoves in the adjoining rooms."

With quick steps she ran into the next room. When she returned a moment later, she continued, "The tiled section is about as wide as the fireplace. Just a minute!" She ran to the door of the other room, looked in and said, "That stove is just as wide. There should be a hollow space about three feet wide between them."

"Could be," agreed Paul. "But that space may have been divided evenly between the two stoves."

"Let's measure it," suggested Katie.

"But how?" Eric asked.

Katie thought hard. "In the olden days, space was measured by using a foot. Let's try that."

"Or by arm length. That's much simpler!" Eric suggested.

"Okay," said Katie. "Let's start over here to the left. Three arm lengths," she announced. "And now the right side."

"Should also be three," said Anne, watching Katie measure.

When Katie finished she announced, "About two and one-third." Then she measured the outer wall: three arm lengths. "Didn't I tell you! There must be an empty space." She pointed to the right.

"If that's true, let's investigate!" Paul grabbed hold of the edge of the opening, jumped up, and climbed inside. Quietly the others watched him as he looked over the right hand side of the storage space. He was about to give up, but looked up once more into the corner. "A hole! But no bar or anything else."

"Use the poker." Eric passed it to him. Barely had

Paul pulled at it with the poker, when he whispered excitedly, "It's moving! There's a spring behind it. Try pressing against the door."

"Wait, I'm coming." Quickly Eric climbed up.

"Okay! I'll use the poker once more, and you watch the wall. Does it move?"

Eric pressed and pushed. Nothing happened. Suddenly Paul yelled, "Push that spot again! Something here was moving."

Eric pushed the wall with the whole weight of his body.

"More!" urged Paul.

"I can't push any harder," Eric grunted.

"Wait, I'll help you." Paul took the poker, pushed it into the tiny crack, turned it, and gave it a hard tug. With a screech a metal door opened up to reveal a dark space from which musty air rose. The boys gasped for breath.

"Quick, the flashlight!" cried Eric. He took it from Rebecca and beamed into the open space.

"Stairs leading down!" he exclaimed. "The secret passage!"

"Come on, what are we waiting for?" Paul reached out his hand to help Katie up.

Eric called from the stairs, "I'm starting down!"

"No!" ordered Anne. "We're all sticking together!"

When all were inside, Paul carefully pulled the door shut and gave orders to Eric: "Forward, march!"

A Knight Points the Way

The children slowly descended the stairs. Rebecca counted eighteen steps. Then the stairs ended, and a tunnel stretched ahead of them. It was about five feet high and three feet wide. The walls glistened with moisture, and the children's footsteps echoed strangely in the tunnel.

"I've got goose bumps! It's spooky here," whispered Rebecca. After about 150 feet the tunnel ended at a solid wall. The children looked at each other helplessly. Eric shined the light on the walls.

"Rock," he mumbled. "What's above us?"

They looked up to see a large rectangular stone slab.

"Come on, let's try to lift the slab," Paul urged.

They all pressed against it with their hands. Nothing happened.

"We aren't going to get anywhere here," Eric said. "This stone slab has two sides. If we look carefully at the direction in which the tunnel runs and measure in steps how long it is, we could tell where it ends."

"Or continues," added Paul.

"Let's go," said Rebecca. "The air in here is so musty that I'm feeling sick. The batteries of the flashlight may not last much longer either."

Carefully the children found their way back. Rebecca was the first to climb out of the stove. She ran into a room overlooking the yard and stood looking out. She tried to measure the direction and length of the passage with her eyes, then ran back to the others.

"Guess where the passage ends?" she asked eagerly.

"Well, are you going to tell?" asked Anne impatiently.

"Probably in the chapel!"

"I get it!" Eric's face beamed. "Remember the flat tombstones on the chapel floor? They're about the size of the stone slab that closed off the passage. Let's find out!"

In the chapel the children stood around helplessly among the many tombstones that were located in the rear of the chapel.

"If only we knew which one it is," Paul said, "or even if it really is one of these slabs."

Anne began stamping lightly with her foot on the stones. "Maybe we can find it by the sound."

"The soles of our shoes are too soft. I'm going for a stick from the fireplace." Rebecca hurried away and returned a moment later with a large piece of wood.

Paul took it and carefully tapped the stone slabs, taking care to do it in spots where there were no inscriptions. Everyone was quiet, listening to the sounds produced. Suddenly they all heard it.

"This slab has a different sound!" Paul exclaimed.

Eric examined the edges. "If it's this slab, it certainly hasn't been lifted up for quite some time. The grooves are full of dust." He scratched the slab. "Hard as rock, and really old!"

Katie was getting impatient. "All right, if this is the slab we're after, we've solved the mystery. We know where the passage ends."

"You said *if*," replied Rebecca. "But suppose this is a different passage or that the passage ends somewhere else?"

"I know!" cried Eric.

"What?" Anne asked.

"The answer! I mean, how we can track down the answer we need! One of us has to go back into the secret passage and knock against the slab from below."*

"Great idea!" Paul looked at his younger brother with admiration. Paul took the stick and the flashlight and was off. A few minutes later the children heard the tapping. They cheered. It was indeed the stone they thought it was.

Anne stamped her foot on the slab a few times to signal to Paul.

When he returned to the chapel, Anne exclaimed, "Yes, that was it!"

"Just a minute! Please hand me the stick." Eric went over to the slabs on the wall and began tapping them.

Paul shook his head. "No need to try that. The walls aren't very thick."

In spite of this Eric continued his tapping, touching each slab. The others watched him patiently.

------

*See map: The secret passage runs from #23 to the chapel (#14).

Suddenly Katie cried, "Hey, try that one again."

Eric tapped again on the slab that was exactly in the center of the wall.

Katie walked out, hurried back into the chapel, and announced, "Paul, you were only partly right about the walls. These three," she said, "are not thick. But this one here," she pointed to the wall in which the strange-sounding slab was situated, "is an extension of the thick castle wall."

Eric whistled through his teeth. "That's very interesting. Paul, come here and stand in front of the slab. I want to get up on your shoulders."

He looked at the top of the stone slab and called out, "There's some kind of secret, that's for sure!"

"What secret?" Paul asked, squirming under the pressure of Eric's shoes digging down into his shoulders.

"All the slabs are held to the wall with two iron hooks, both top and bottom." He looked around at the other slabs. "I can see the holes into which these hooks have been cemented. But this slab is different."

"How? Hurry!" groaned Paul.

"The hooks don't go into the wall, but down behind the slab."

"See anything else?"

"No, the slab is too close to the wall."

"Come down—now!" Paul grunted.

Eric jumped down. "Am I really that heavy?"

"Not really, but the soles of your shoes have sharp edges." Paul rubbed his shoulders. "I think I'll live in spite of the pain!"

Katie bent down to feel the bottom edge of the stone. "It seems to be the same here," she said. "The iron disappears behind the edge and doesn't end in the wall."

Carefully the children looked at all the grooves between the wall and the slab, but found nothing.

Katie noticed that Eric was examining another stone slab, at the far side of the wall. "Something there?"

"I don't know," said Eric. "The slab over there has a half-inch crack in the middle of it. It's about five inches long."

"This time have someone else lift you up there," muttered Paul. "If the iron hooks are cemented into the slab, the stone won't move."

The children came closer and inspected the tombstone. A knight in full armor was carved into the stone. His right foot rested on a dragon-like animal. His bent arm rested on his knee. His left hand grasped a lance.

Eric approached the slab, set his foot on part of the carved animal, and said, "Please give me a boost up!"

Katie and Rebecca helped him up.

"I see a piece of metal there," Eric called out, "and I can move it a bit. It seems to be a lever."

Eric climbed down, and Anne returned to the slab at the center. "Come back here. Maybe luck is with us."

The children pulled at the right side. Nothing happened. Rebecca wanted to give up when Eric suggested, "Let's try the other side." They had just begun to pull when the entire slab moved toward them. With astonishment the children were looking into a dark opening below.

"Another secret passage!" cried Eric.

Anne stepped up to the opening and called out, "Be careful, it goes straight down. The passage turns left after about four feet, and then there are steps leading down. Where's the light?"

"Here!" Paul said. "Unfortunately it won't do you much good. I could see almost nothing by it when I was in the other secret passage. We need a stronger light."

"Oh, no!" groaned Katie, "and this is Saturday, and all the stores will be closed by now."

"Why not try it without the light?" Eric asked.

"No," decided Anne. "We don't know where it leads. Better to be kept in suspense than to end up in a hospital!"

When the stone slab had been replaced in the wall and the secret bolt fastened again, Anne noticed something strange.

"Look!" she said. "The tip of the knight's lance points directly to the hidden bolt."

"And where the foot of the rider is, Eric set his foot in order to step up and reach the bolt," Katie observed.

"I see something else," Anne said. "The knight's right hand points in the direction of the center door. And look at his fingers. The thumb and forefinger are bent, but the small, ring, and middle fingers point toward the secret passage."

"Neat!" said Paul. "There sure was a lot of imagination at work here!"

"It's simple," declared Eric, "once you know the secret."

*　　*　　*

During supper the phone rang. Katie answered. "It's Dad!" she called to the others. They crowded around the phone, everyone eager to talk with him. Rebecca immediately shared the news of their latest discovery, explaining how the knight pointed to the secret passage. Both parents were impressed.

"I'll call again in a couple of days," their father

said. "Then you can tell me where that new passage leads."

The Underground Passage

W hen the five Bakers went down to the village the next morning to attend church service, they saw a couple in front of the church. The woman was the clerk Paul and Eric had met at the electronics shop. When she spotted the two boys, she waved and called to them. "I told my husband about you. He was surprised—and impressed."

The man smiled warmly. "You're coming for the service?" he asked.

The children nodded. Then into Anne's mind flashed the solution to their flashlight problem! This couple owns an electronics shop; they would have flashlight batteries.

She spoke up quickly. "We ran out of flashlight batteries yesterday. This afternoon we'd like to do something important, and we need some new batteries. Would it be possible for you to sell us some batteries after church?"

"Yes, we'll be glad to help you," the woman said. "Come with us after the close of the service."

The church bells began to ring. The man called

out to them, "Come, the service has already begun."

The children followed him, happy that the problem of the batteries would be solved.

After the service, they hurried to meet the couple again. Together they went toward the shop.

To make conversation Katie asked, "Why did you say before, when the bells were beginning to ring, that the service had already started?"

"Here many people leave their homes when the bells begin to ring. But that's wrong. Bells are not rung to get people away from their homes. Their sound is a call to prayer. Those church members who are unable to attend church can pray at home at the same time that everyone else does. There is a real blessing resting in those first ten minutes while the bells are ringing," the man added. "People in the church put everyday things aside and prepare for worship."

Soon the group reached the electronics shop. Inside, the woman asked, "What kind of batteries do you need?"

Paul walked over to the counter, picked up six batteries, and asked, "How much are these?"

"That's a hard question," replied the man. "For me Sunday is a day of rest on which I never do any business or work. Therefore I cannot sell you the batteries."

The children looked at the couple helplessly. Then they noticed the mischievous twinkle in the man's eyes.

His wife nudged him, saying, "You shouldn't lead the children on so! Tell them what you mean."

The man laughed. "Because I can't sell them today, I must give them to you!"

The Baker children sighed in relief, said their

thank yous, and returned to the castle.

As soon as the lunch dishes were washed and dried, they were off. Paul was already waiting on the castle grounds, flashlight in hand. The children went first to the main building, then quietly slipped into the chapel. Eric slid the secret bolt, and together the children moved the heavy stone door. With hearts pounding they entered the secret tunnel, which turned left and then descended. After they had used an iron handle on the inside of the door to close it, they carefully felt their way down the wet stone steps. Paul hurried ahead.

"Not so fast!" Anne protested. "Shine the light back here so we can see something."

The steps led them farther down. The light shining on the ceiling revealed large drops of water on the hewn stone.

"Wait a minute!" whispered Katie. "I need to catch my breath."

"You're not a grandmother!" mocked Eric.

"Oh, you! I just need time to get used to this spooky place!"

"The air here is fresher than in the last passage," Anne observed.

"How come?" Katie asked. "Fresh air is possible only if there's some movement of the air."

"We'll find out soon," Paul said. "Down there the stairs end."

At the bottom there was a larger, more level passage.

Paul stopped. "No doubt about it," he said. "The tunnel leads to the outside."

"How do you know?" Anne asked.

"Back there the tunnel turned left, then the steps went down. So we're now just below the western tower."

"He's right," agreed Katie.

"This passage," said Paul, pointing ahead, "dips slightly. It must go down below the castle walls, under the moat, and then beyond the castle."*

"Let's go ahead," suggested Eric.

After about a hundred feet the tunnel ended. A circular staircase led upward. On the left was a stone slab. A family coat of arms underneath a Latin inscription had been engraved upon it.

Rebecca deciphered the words, "Lapis, Grandstein." She mumbled the words as if to herself, then moved on, feeling her way up the steps. Suddenly daylight flooded the passage. After a few more yards, the children stood at a gun hole and were surprised to see the drawbridge and the open castle gate.*

Eric hurried up a few more steps but came right down again. "Two more gun holes ahead. You can see the castle gate through both of them."

"I get it!" Anne said. "It's like the layout we found at Castle Gutenberg on the Neckar River. If the castle had to be defended, it was possible to fire at the enemy from these gun holes while they were attempting to build a temporary bridge or trying to break down the drawbridge and the castle gate."

"A good design," agreed Eric. "They were safe in the tower here with thick walls all around, and above them a solid stone ceiling."

"The castle gate was the most vulnerable spot in the castle, because nobody would try to cross the moat and climb up the steep surrounding walls,

---

*See map: #14 and #15, when connected, show the direction of the secret tunnel.

---

*See map: The children are in the Outer Tower (#9).

especially while being fired at from the walls above," explained Paul.

"It's easy to see why this castle was never invaded or destroyed," agreed Rebecca.

"But suppose someone had broken in through the walls of the towers?" Eric asked.

"Not very likely, when the walls are ten feet thick," Paul said. "The weakest points were the gun holes, but they could be defended by shooting from the towers. If the attacker did succeed in entering the tower and the passage, what good would it do? From the chapel the steep, narrow staircase could easily have been defended, or the stone slab could have been rammed shut. It was impossible to invade the castle, and the enemy would know it."

"We're at the end of this tunnel and yet at the beginning," Anne said.

Eric looked at her, not understanding what she meant. "Well, we have found a passage that leads outside the castle, but no one could have left the castle through this tunnel without being seen."

"Come on, let's move on," Paul said, shining the light on the steps and leading the way down the circular staircase.

When they reached the bottom, Eric suggested, "Why don't we try to figure out the words on the slab."

The children read: "Dominus Jesus Christus monia laeta et prospera precetur, ne quid detrimenti capiatis, sed laeti fortunatique intro quas parietinas sitis."

"Please translate," Anne said to Rebecca. "You took Latin for three years."

"May Jesus Christ bless you," Rebecca read

slowly, "that no harm may strike you, but be happy and cheerful within these walls." She sighed, "I don't know if my Latin teacher would have given me a good grade for that translation, but that's the sense of the words. How would you translate them, Paul?"

"Same as you did," he answered.

While the others had been working at the translation, Eric was studying the slab. He noticed that some of the letters had been engraved more deeply than others. He pointed them out, "Do you notice the c,u,n,i,c,u,l,u,s?"

"Hey!" cried Rebecca. "That's a Latin word!"

"Maybe it's just a coincidence," suggested Anne. "What does it mean?"

"Cuniculus...cuniculus...let's see. Oh, I know!"

"Well, what does it mean?" Anne asked.

"Something like 'underground passage.'"

Eric stepped forward. "Paul, please lift me up. I'd like to see the upper edge of the slab."

"Why?"

"Don't you understand? Think back to the directions in the chapel."

Paul caught on. "Hop up!"

In a few seconds Eric was up on Paul's shoulders, lighting up the top of the stone with his flashlight. Suddenly he shouted, "I've got it! There's a handle here. I'll turn it." Quickly he jumped from Paul's shoulders and grasped the side of the stone slab. Slowly the stone moved on its hinges, revealing a dark opening. A spiral staircase led downward.

"I can hardly wait!" whispered Rebecca. "Maybe this is finally the tunnel we've been looking for so long—the *real* secret passage!"

Eric's eyes gleamed with anticipation. He took

the flashlight. "Come on, this time I'm going ahead!"

After two complete turns the stairs ended. A passage lay straight ahead, but leading steeply downward with steps here and there. Slowly the children made their way down. The walls were moist, the rock beneath their feet slick.

"Hurry, the light is growing dim!" Eric cried.

"I don't see how that can happen. The batteries are almost new," Paul said.

Eric stopped. "It's no use, we have to go back. Something is wrong with this flashlight."

"No way!" answered Paul. "Even if we fall or have to crawl back in the darkness, we're going on!"

Anne disagreed. "Eric is right."

"You're just scared!" Paul snapped.

Anne shook her head. "Since when is being careful the same as being scared?"

Paul ignored her and moved ahead. "Look, up ahead the tunnel makes a turn. I'll run ahead to see whether there's something special coming up."

"Okay, go on," Anne said, watching the beam of light as Paul hurried ahead. Suddenly something about it puzzled her. The light had disappeared. A minute later it was coming back toward them.

"Quick, come over here!" yelled Paul. "There's a second passage here branching off from this one."

Curiosity made them all move. The passage continued with a slight bend to the right. Then a second tunnel branched off at a 90-degree angle. Both tunnels sloped steeply downward.

Paul switched off the light, and the children stood in the darkness to decide on their next move.

"I don't understand this," Paul complained.

"These batteries should last much longer." He switched the light on again. This time the light was stronger.

"Hurray!" called Paul. "Now, which way do we go?" Again he switched off the light.

"Who knows what else is ahead," said Katie. "Maybe it would be better if one of us stayed here and waited while the others went on."

"Okay," agreed Rebecca. "Since you suggested it, are you volunteering to stay?"

Katie was not enthusiastic, but she mumbled, "Sure, get going!"

In places the tunnel became very narrow. The going was slippery. A coating of mud and clay had been washed down through the cracks in the rocks.

Rebecca lost her footing and landed in a dirty puddle. Her jacket and slacks were covered with mud. "Look at me!" she complained.

Carefully the children felt their way onward. The sides of the tunnel became even wetter, and drops of moisture glistened on the rock above. Puddles lay in the low places.

Paul stopped. "I'd sure like to know how much farther this goes."

"I'm not quitting," Rebecca announced. "I can't get much dirtier than I am right now!"

"Then let's go ahead," Anne agreed.

After another five minutes the passage seemed to end.

"Clogged up with mud and sand! Just our luck!" Paul shined the light upward, revealing a big opening in the rock above. Apparently dirt had fallen down, blocking the tunnel.

"Well, at least now we know where the passage

ends!" Rebecca declared.*

"But not where it used to end," interrupted Eric.

"Well, we still have the other tunnel," Rebecca added.

"Sure," answered Paul wearily. "Let's go back."

The way back was easier, and the children quickly covered the distance.

"Finally!" Katie snapped. "I'm freezing just standing around here in the dark."

"At least you're clean," Rebecca said, showing her sister her muddy clothes.

Anne walked a few steps into the passage they hadn't yet explored. Suddenly she slipped on a wet stone, tried to steady herself, and knocked the flashlight against the rocky wall so hard that the light went out.

The children all groaned as Anne felt her way back to the group.

Paul inspected the light. "Can't do a thing about it! The bulb must be broken. Well, let's get on with it."

Slowly and carefully, falling and sliding, they found their way back. When they came to the chapel, they slouched exhausted in the pews.

"So, what happens now?" Katie asked.

"That's obvious," Eric said. "Tomorrow we buy five new flashlights, extra batteries and bulbs, and get to the end of the second secret passage."

"Tomorrow is right!" answered Rebecca. "I've had enough for today."

---

*See map: #9 and #2 connected show the direction of this tunnel. The fork is at #2. Note: The secret passage led from the fork to the rubble heap at #3.

An Important Discovery

The next morning the children prepared for a renewed search of the tunnels. Paul and Rebecca had gone into town early to buy flashlights and batteries. At nine all were ready to take off. The rubber boots, bought for rainy days, were coming in handy. The children took their careful roundabout route to the main building. Quickly they reached the secret passage, and moved cautiously through the steep, slippery tunnel.

When they paused to catch their breath, Anne said, "Today the tunnel doesn't look nearly as eerie as it did yesterday."

"With five flashlights everything is much lighter too!" Rebecca added.

"What do we do if this passage is also closed up?" Katie asked.

Paul shook his head. "Let's worry about that when we're actually standing on the pile of rocks and dirt."

"He's right," Rebecca said. "We'll take care of that when it comes." She started off again. The others followed.

At the fork in the tunnel Katie recalled, "This is where I stood yesterday—freezing and afraid in the dark."

At first the new tunnel led steeply downward. Suddenly Katie stopped and shined her light into the darkness. "There's a reflection down there. Oh-oh, the tunnel is filled with water. We can't get through that."

All five children paused.

"Go on," urged Eric. "Maybe it isn't very deep."

He was right. The water was only seven or eight inches deep. Carefully the children waded through it.

Paul stopped. "You know what I think?" Without waiting for someone to answer, he continued. "I think we're at the level of the lake."

"There's something I don't understand," said Anne. "If the passage continues in this direction, it will end in the lake or at the shore. But we searched that whole area thoroughly and didn't see any opening."

"Not the whole area," replied Eric. "We were not in the mill!"

"Man, you're right!" Rebecca exclaimed. "It could be! Let's go." She splashed her way through the water with the others following.

After another fifty feet the floor level rose and the water receded. Suddenly the children found themselves in front of a door.

"The end!" Rebecca said, disappointed.

"Maybe it can be opened." Eric suggested.

Paul flashed his light around the edges. "There's not much we can do. The lock must be on the other side."

In his frustration he kicked the door. With a

crunch a rotten board broke and fell with a damp thud. The children looked anxiously at the dark opening. When everything remained quiet, Paul carefully shined his light through the hole.

"Steps leading up!" Before the others could respond, Paul pushed his way quickly through the hole. After a few seconds he called, "The door has only one bolt, but it's covered with rust."

Still the others stood motionless.

Paul called again, "Well, come on! There haven't been people here for ages. The rusted bolt is proof of that."

The other children crawled through the splintered door. Narrow stone steps led upward for about thirty feet. Then a heavy wooden ceiling covered the passage. Eric pushed against it. Nothing moved.

"Looks like a trapdoor," Rebecca suggested.

"I think it's a regular cellar door," Katie said. "If we all push on it with our shoulders, and there's no bolt on the other side, maybe we can open it."

All five lined themselves up on the steps in order to push against the door. After only one try the door opened with a creaking sound. In the next moment something heavy crashed onto the ceiling above them.

"Down!" whispered Paul. Quickly the children lowered the door and listened anxiously. Nothing moved.

"What can we do?" whispered Anne in the darkness.

"We'll just wait to find out if anyone heard us and is coming over here," Paul said.

"There's a difference between hearing and coming," answered Katie. "If someone heard us, he might not come right away. He might be waiting to see what we'll do."

"I think one thing is certain," Eric said. "I saw a room above the cellar door. So we must be below the old mill. There is no other building in this direction for miles. And the mill is empty."

"How do you know?" asked Rebecca. "We haven't had a look at the small sticks we placed in front of the doors. Also, remember the car in the garage."

Anne became impatient. "I think we should do what we did last year in the secret cellar. Eric stays near the rotten door. Rebecca waits on the steps here. I stay in the room above us. And Katie and Paul search the building. If there's some danger, there are two ways of escaping and getting help!"

"Good!" Let's do it that way!" Paul agreed. "Let's lift the cellar door again."

Soon the door was raised. The girls held it while the boys scrambled up, opened it wide, and laid the door down on the floor.

"Now, everyone to their assigned posts," whispered Anne.

Katie and Paul looked around the room. Only a little light came in through the dust-covered window.

Katie pointed to a stool that lay on its side on the floor. "That's what caused the crash! It was probably standing on the cellar door," she said.

Except for a table, the room was empty.

Paul carefully opened the door to the room, looked out, and whispered, "It's the mill all right!"

"Do you see anyone?" Anne called.

"No," Paul said, "but with all the machinery in here, there are a million places to hide."

"I know!" said Anne from her place on the steps. "One of you could climb out through the window and check the small sticks. Then we'd know if someone had entered the mill."

"Right!" Paul hurried over to the window, opened it, and jumped down. After a minute he was back. "Everything's okay!" he announced. "Both sticks are still in place. We've got the mill to ourselves."

Katie, Rebecca, and Anne came up into the room. With awe they inspected the huge cogwheels among the rafters above, then went upstairs. The boys looked at the worn millstones.

Paul touched the huge lever, which had been used to lead the water of the stream over the waterwheel. "Hey Eric, give me a hand with this," he called.

The huge waterwheel began to move, the millstones turned, and the rafters shuddered and creaked. Quickly Paul and Eric pushed the lever back. Immediately everything was still again.

With pale faces the girls came running down.

"What was that? I thought the whole place was coming down!" Rebecca exclaimed.

After Paul explained, she asked, "How do we get to the garage?"

The others shrugged their shoulders. They couldn't see any door.

Anne carefully looked over the wall of boards. She pointed upward and said, "Look, a sliding door! Come on, help me."

The children pushed the door open. There was a dark room, and in it a station wagon.

Rebecca ran immediately to look at the license plate. "Oh-oh!" she exclaimed. "Paul, I think you need a trip to the eye doctor!"

"What? Why?"

"Well, what did you tell us was on the license plates?"

"RUB-PX."

"Have a look! The letters are RUD-PX."

"I don't need an eye doctor," Paul said defensively. "In the first place, it was dark in here. And I couldn't see that there was a screw in the middle of the D, making it look like a B. The annual sticker is missing, so that car probably has not been driven for years. Also notice the four flat tires."

After the children explored the old mill for another hour, Katie reminded them, "This afternoon there's a youth class at the church in the village. We still have to have lunch and clean up."

"Right! We'll have to go!" Anne agreed. Before the children closed the cellar door, Katie pointed out, "See how carefully the door is hidden in the pattern? The entire floor is divided into equal rectangles, so nobody would suspect a door. Who would even imagine that one of the rectangles was movable?"*

When the children returned to the chapel, they closed up the passage with the stone slab.

Rebecca breathed a sigh of relief. "Wow, that was quite a walk! What are we going to make for lunch?"

"We'll think of something," answered Anne.

No one suspected that two eyes were watching them through a crack in the altar at the side of the chapel, that two ears were listening carefully to every word they said.

* * *

---

*See map: The tunnel leads from the fork (#2) into the mill (#1).

At the youth class the five Bakers felt very comfortable. After a few songs, a Bible study, and a prayer, the group played some games. Then there was a Bible quiz with prizes for the winners.

After the classes the children went to see the Martins. Frau Martin said to them, "I am surprised at how well you're getting along without your parents here. I was expecting you to ask for help. Your parents will be pleased to hear how you're doing."

"They already know," Rebecca said. "We talk to them on the phone every other day."

"Tell me," continued Frau Martin. "Have you read the newspaper reports of your adventure?"

The children shook their heads.

"I think you might enjoy seeing them. A woman in our church collected all of them. After coffee you could go over there and see her. I'm sure she'd be pleased to have you come!"

"Oh, great!" cried Anne. "I'd like to see those clippings."

After a half hour the five Bakers, together with the three Martin boys, were on their way.

They were greeted at the door by an elderly lady. "I'm glad you've come! I have a surprise for you. Everything that was written about you in the newspapers or magazines! I saved every bit!" She brought out all the clippings.

"This isn't a good picture of me," Anne protested.

When no one responded to her comment, she turned to Paul and repeated it. He looked up and mumbled, "I think that picture flatters you."

"Well, so much for you!" Anne said, and grabbed another clipping.

After some time Katie leaned back and said, "These reports are very interesting, but they don't tell about all the problems and fears we had before we found the treasure."

"Is the old castle still an interesting place for you even now?" asked the woman.

"Oh, yes," replied Rebecca. "There's always something to discover."

"Another treasure maybe?"

"Well, we can't really say that. We have no evidence of one so far."

Katie noticed an oil painting of the castle hanging on the wall. "That looks very romantic!"

"It not only looks romantic, it is from the Romantic Period, about 150 years ago. It is a family heirloom," answered their hostess.

"Just look how those leaves and clouds were painted," exclaimed Rebecca. "And here, the children playing with their dog. Everything looks like a dream."

"Unfortunately, about two years ago, a relative knocked the picture off the wall and it fell on the corner of a chair. An artist repaired the hole and did it very well, as you can see."

That remark awakened Anne's interest. "I supposed he glued something to the back of the painting."

"Yes, he did," replied the woman. She took the painting from the wall and turned it over."

"Oh, a second canvas," said Rebecca.

"You can see both—the old and the new," the woman said.

The children thanked the lady for an interesting visit and then left.

"Now, tell me quickly," Andreas said to Paul.

"Have you discovered anything important at the castle?"

"We sure have!" exclaimed Paul. "A secret tunnel! It runs from the castle to the mill."

"To the mill?"

"Yes," replied Eric. "It ends in a side room under a hidden cellar door."

"Fantastic! Day after tomorrow we're coming over. Will you show it to us?" Markus asked.

"Of course!" Paul said.

Dangerous Undertakings

Eric and Katie had gone to town early in the morning. Now the children were at the breakfast table, enjoying the fresh rolls. Paul and Eric liked theirs with jam or honey; the girls preferred cheese or sausage.

"We've been here for more than a week now," Paul said. "We've had some interesting experiences, but I wonder what else will happen. I'm glad that Herr Grabinsky has turned out to be an honest man. I'm not expecting any new adventures with him. Today I'd like to read a book, and my diary has lots of empty pages."

"And there are lots of empty postcards staring me in the face," Anne said. "I should be sending them to my friends."

Suddenly Rebecca motioned toward Eric. He was sitting there motionless, his mouth full of bread, staring into space. The sudden silence around him awoke him from his dreams. Startled, he looked around at the others.

"Well, good morning!" teased Anne. "I think

our little brother should go to bed earlier in the evening!"

"It doesn't make any sense!" Eric muttered. He walked slowly over to one of the paintings in the dining room and carefully looked at its back side.

Katie was curious and came over to him. "Did you figure out something new?"

Eric showed the others the back of the oil painting and asked, "Did the paintings in the Knights' Hall look like this?" He tapped the canvas that peeked out between the wedge and the picture frame.

"Yes, I think they did," Rebecca replied.

"The painting we saw last night at the friendly lady's house was different!" Eric announced.

"Well, certainly," answered Rebecca quickly, "It had a second canvas." Suddenly she slapped a hand to her forehead. "I get it! Grabinsky wanted to convince us that there was a second canvas behind those paintings. I think we do have a band of counterfeit painters on our hands, after all!"

"Careful now," warned Anne, "we don't have any proof. We shouldn't be suspicious of honest people!"

"Let's find out!" Katie called and jumped up.

"Stop," cried Anne. "We should plan carefully, so we don't make mistakes."

Paul agreed with her. "If we're right, then the visit to the museum was a maneuver to distract our attention and lead us astray."

After a long discussion the five Bakers agreed that the two boys should have another look at the paintings.

"Wait, I just thought of something else." Rebecca raised her hand. "It could be that there really is a second canvas, but that it can't be seen."

Anne wrinkled her brow. "What do you mean?"

"Well, that gold-covered, decorative frame could be hiding the old, smaller canvas."

"Hmmm," mumbled Paul. "No problem! In the closet we have a hammer and a pair of pliers. We'll take them with us. If necessary, we'll pull the tacks or nails from the frame and remove the painting. Then we'll be able to see."

"Another thing!" Eric looked over at the girls. "If we're not back in fifteen minutes, you know what to do."

Katie and Rebecca nodded.

"Just a minute!" called Anne, "I've just remembered that in our excitement we forgot our morning prayers. We'd better take care of that first."

After the prayers the boys left the house, and the girls settled down in easy chairs without a word. The minutes ticked by.

"What if the paintings really are counterfeit?" Anne asked. "What do we do then?"

"Call Inspector Martin," responded Rebecca immediately.

Katie wriggled uncomfortably in her chair. "Yes and no! I think we should do the detective work ourselves. Later the police can do the arresting."

"Detective work?" Anne asked.

"Yes! For instance, we don't even know where the entrance to their painting area is and..."

"I'm getting nervous," Anne interrupted. She jumped up and went over to the window.

"The boys have been gone for more than ten minutes."

"Twelve minutes," announced Rebecca, staring at her watch.

Katie also got up and went to stand at the window. Without a word the two sisters looked down at the castle grounds.

"Fourteen minutes!" Rebeccá crossed over to the telephone.

"Don't call yet! Just wait!" Anne said nervously.

After a bit Rebecca declared, "Sixteen minutes! I'm calling!" Katie and Anne listened as she dialed. After about a minute she put the receiver down. There was no answer! A cold hand of fear clutched the girls.

Katie gave Anne a worried look. "What are we going to do if the boys have been captured and we're being watched?"

"We'll just wait," said Anne. "No one can come in here. Tawny wouldn't allow them. And sooner or later the Martins have to come home."

"Maybe Inspector Martin is on duty," suggested Katie.

"Hey, that's the solution," cried Rebecca. "Let's call the police!"

* * *

Meanwhile the two boys had carefully entered the Knights' Hall and taken one painting from the wall. Paul pulled the tiny nails from the heavy decorated wooden frame, which contained the inner frame on which the canvas was stretched.

"These nails are suspiciously loose," he whispered. Barely had the last nail been pulled and the inner frame removed, when both boys saw that there was indeed only one canvas. They checked another painting and found the same thing. Just as the brothers were about ready to rehang the paintings, they heard voices from the stairwell.

"Quick!" whispered Eric. In a few seconds the

job was completed. Without making a sound they listened.

* * *

Rebecca had just gone back to the phone when Katie called, "There they are!"

"At last!" Anne murmured.

"Are they alone?"

When Anne and Rebecca assured her that the boys were alone, Katie put down the receiver.

The boys came in and went straight for the easy chairs. The girls waited in suspense.

"Well, what's wrong?" asked Katie.

Eric said nothing, but held up one finger.

"What's that supposed to mean?" Rebecca asked impatiently.

"Only one canvas! We inspected two paintings."

"And guess what this means!" Paul held out a brown finger.

"Dirt?" Anne guessed.

Her brother shook his head. "Paint, my dear sister. Wet paint from a painting, which according to the brass plaque on it, is more than 200 years old!"

"That Grabinsky!" exclaimed Katie. "Tricking his own uncle!"

"Why were you gone so long?" Rebecca asked.

Paul told the girls about their work and the voices they had heard.

"And then what?" asked Katie.

"Well, we crept over to the door to listen," Eric said. "Only we couldn't get a word they said. The door was closed, and the echo in the staircase covered up the words. But it sounded like they were very excited."

"That's why it took so long," explained Paul. "We didn't dare move into the stairwell. When one man —I think it was Grabinsky—finally came down and went across the hall to his place, we hurried back."

"We have to find out where the entrance to that painting workshop is," said Eric, thinking aloud. "Maybe one of us could hide somewhere in the attic to see if someone goes in or out a secret door."

"We could do that," agreed Katie, "but which of us would be willing to wait hours and hours for Grabinsky?"

Eric had another proposal. "We could go up together and make a really thorough search of the attic."

"That sounds better," said Katie. "Let's go!"

The children left the house and climbed into the attic.

"Now," Katie said, "behind those two thick walls there is a very steep decline. Nothing important there. So there are only the parts with the slanting roofs left. On this side the building is two stories lower. So that leaves only those slanting roof areas."

"The area behind that we already searched last year," Paul recalled.

"I remember, but there's no other possibility," Katie said.

The children went over everything very carefully, pushing and pulling at boards and beams and walls. Nothing moved!

Paul opened the lid of a huge chest. It was empty. *A good hiding place*, he thought with a slight shudder. He noticed that none of the others was watching him at the moment, so he quickly climbed in and carefully let down the lid. There was a loud click.

"Where's Paul?" whispered Eric.

The girls looked at each other. Suddenly the lid of the chest began slowly to open. With staring eyes the four stood watching. When they saw Paul, a sigh of relief went up.

Katie came over to ask, "How did you open the lock from the inside?"

"Simple," Paul explained. "The lock presses against this spring and opens it. I just pulled at the spring."

"Come over here," Katie called quietly to the others. "This is a perfect hiding place."

"But," Rebecca interrupted, "if you're discovered, it makes a perfect trap!"

"No," said Katie, defending her idea. "Unless a person had the key, he couldn't open it. And it would be impossible to carry the huge chest away."

Eric peeked in. "You're sure the lock can be opened from the inside?"

Paul demonstrated how easily it could be done.

"A very simple lock," Eric observed.

"True," agreed Paul, "but only if the key fits. Look at the notches on the lock more carefully. Every notch is important. I bet the key that opens this is the same one that opens the castle doors and gates. Otherwise, there's no way to get in."

"The chest is so huge," Anne said. "Two of us could easily hide in it at once. It would be great to have company!"

"Sure would!" Katie looked around at her brothers and sisters. "Who volunteers to stay first?"

"Why not you?" Paul asked.

Katie gulped.

"I'll keep you company," volunteered Rebecca. "Who'll take the next turn?"

Anne looked at her watch. "It's now 10:30. How

about 1 P.M.? The next two can come just after lunch, and you wouldn't be very late for yours."

"Sounds good!" Katie said.

"Take the key in with you," advised Paul. "Put it in between the chest and the lid. That will leave a crack to spy through. In case of real danger, you simply pull the key away and the chest will be locked."

Back in their apartment, Paul, Eric, and Anne got busy preparing lunch.

"It's a good thing there are five of us," said Eric.

"Why?" asked Anne.

"Well," he said. "Two are keeping watch. If they're discovered, and the two who are supposed to take their place are also captured, that still leaves one of us at home who can call the police."

"You're right! It *is* a good thing there are five of us."

The hours went by. While two of the children were hiding in the trunk, the others spent their time writing to friends, reading, and playing games. Every few hours a new pair took a turn in the trunk.

At 8:30 P.M. something happened. Paul and Eric already had kept watch for more than two hours and were waiting for Katie and Rebecca, who were to watch for the last two hours, when they heard footsteps in the stairwell! Quickly the two boys climbed back into the chest and lowered the lid, leaving the crack to watch through.

The footsteps came closer. Then a door opened, and a man entered. It was Grabinsky. He went over to a certain place in the slanting ceiling, removed two huge nails from a rafter, put his weight against it, and moved a part of the ceiling to one side, revealing a narrow place. He ducked and crawled in, closed the opening, and the boys could hear him going down some stairs. They heard another door open with a loud creaking sound, and then two voices. But soon all was quiet again.

Paul playfully punched his brother's arm. "We've discovered the secret of the hidden room! Now what do we do?"

"Should we leave now?" Eric asked.

Paul consulted his watch. "The girls will be coming any minute."

"Right! Come on, let's meet them!" Eric said.

Barely had they lifted the lid when they again heard voices. Not knowing what to do, they just stood in the chest for a moment. Then they quickly kneeled down and closed the lid.*

"I hope Katie and Rebecca are not on their way up," whispered Paul.

Three men entered the room. They were talking loudly.

The boys heard the sound of Grabinsky's voice. "This is Tuesday. You need two more days, so the paintings can be picked up on Friday."

"And the money?" asked one of the men.

"You get it immediately."

"No money, no paintings!" the man replied.

"And on Saturday we leave this awful prison," said a third voice.

The voices moved, and now were coming through the open door of the stairwell.

"Those kids!" hissed Grabinsky, and the boys could hear his hatred. "How I'd love to take care of them once and for all."

"Hey, some of those kids are coming up! Quickly!"

*See map: #19 and #22 should be connected. Halfway between these two points is the old chest.

99

The men hurried over to the opening, climbed back through, and closed the door again.

"Hurry!" whispered Paul. Like lightning the two boys lifted the lid again, crawled out, tiptoed across the floor and started down the stairs.

Rebecca and Katie stared at them. The boys put their fingers to their lips and pointed anxiously upward. The girls were frightened but hurried down the stairs with the boys.

Once they were down, Paul called in a loud, playful voice, "Just come on out! I saw you. One, two, three! I caught all three of you!"

The two girls stared at Paul. Had he taken leave of his senses? He ran by them into the castle grounds. Shaking their heads, they followed him. As soon as the door of the apartment closed behind them, they peppered the boys with questions.

"Wait a minute," said Eric. "I have to sit down! My knees are still knocking together."

Then, slowly, the boys told their story. The girls listened without moving.

"So they need two more days," said Katie. "We'll see that their plans don't work out! I move that we call Inspector Martin tomorrow morning!"

Eavesdropping!

The next morning, breakfast was later than usual in the apartment. The planned call to Police Inspector Martin heightened the tension.

Meanwhile Grabinsky had driven into town and gone into the only store that sold sports and hobby equipment. He was just inspecting a fine paint brush, when the young clerk came over and wished him a cheerful "Good morning!"

"Morning," grumbled Grabinsky.

"Are the children still at the castle?" the clerk asked.

"Yes, there are children at the castle."

"I mean the ones that were there last year," the clerk tried again. "The treasure hunters!"

"Oh, them! Yes, they are still there. I'll take these two brushes."

"Do you know where they go fishing?"

"No! How much for the brushes?"

"The price is on the box." As he counted out the change, the clerk added, "Strange! They bought our two longest fishing rods, but I have never seen

101

them fishing at the lake. The day they bought the first rod, they told me they didn't really want to catch fish, but words and voices!"

Grabinsky froze. The clerk was so happy to finally have the attention of his customer that he continued. "They told me that—as if it were a secret. They wanted to fish for voices, they said. I think that was a joke. Then they came back the next day and bought the other rod."

"Another rod?" The face of the art student became thoughtful. "Did they say anything else?"

"No."

"Well, who knows what nonsense lies behind those words. Good-bye!"

Grabinsky hurried out of the shop but stopped after a few steps. *Voices?* he thought. *Were those two too loud? I'd better try to find out!*

He continued toward the only electronics store in the town. Entering the store, he said to the owner, "I'd like some flashlight batteries, and... Oh, I've forgotten what else. Do you know those five American children who are spending their vacation at the castle?"

"Yes, certainly!" answered the shop owner.

"Were they here lately?"

"Yes."

"Do you remember what they bought?"

"Yes, batteries and a long microphone cord."

"Oh, I see. Well, I had better pay for these batteries."

Slowly Grabinsky drove back to the castle, all the while planning a terrible scheme.

As he drove across the castle grounds, Katie got up from the breakfast table and watched him through the window. "There's Grabinsky. This will be his last trip in here."

Grabinsky started to enter his quarters, but stopped for a moment, then went outside again and sauntered, as if bored, in the direction of the Baker apartment. Quietly he crept from one window to another. Underneath the dining room window he stopped. He could hear Katie's voice clearly.

"This will be an easy one for the police," she was saying. "The two art counterfeiters will be surprised when the police enter their workshop and they get handcuffs instead of money. Too bad we can't reach Inspector Martin today. Why did he have to go to a conference just now?"

"That's a good question," Rebecca said. "He couldn't know what we were planning. Besides, we could have asked for his substitute to make the arrests."

"No!" cried Katie. "It must be Herr Martin!"

"We still have a day to go," Eric reminded them. "The paintings are to be delivered Friday."

Grabinsky had heard enough. In his excitement he took two quick steps, and the gravel crunched under his feet. Tawny's ears perked up. She bounded to the window with a low growl. The children ran to the window in time to see a cat running along the castle wall.

"Hey, look at that cat over there!" Rebecca pointed to the animal. "Maybe it's the same cat we met last year."

Tawny's growls became more threatening.

"Be quiet!" Paul took the dog's head in his arms. "A big dog like you is not allowed to hurt a little cat."

Grabinsky was still standing near the window, hugging the wall, his face ashen. When the children started to clear the table, he took advantage of the

clatter of the dishes and left.

Around noon a heavy rain began falling. It stopped in the late afternoon and Anne announced, "I'm going for a walk. After a rain there's such a lovely smell in the woods. Anyone coming with me?"

Everyone wanted to go, but after a half hour the children turned back to the castle. Their usual cheerfulness was lacking, because their minds were not on the walk. Even the dog seemed to sense this. She walked slowly behind them, her tail between her legs.

The children crossed the outer courtyard to the door of their apartment and from there noticed Grabinsky hurrying across the inner yard. Just before he reached the door of his living quarters, he stopped, turned his head, and yelled, "You'll pay for this!" He stomped toward them. "You have destroyed priceless treasures!" he shouted.

Anne was the first to speak. "What are you talking about?"

"What am I talking about? Don't act so innocent! You won't get away with this! Your footprints are clearly visible!"

"Where?" asked Katie.

"You were in the chapel, weren't you?"

"Yes," answered Rebecca. "Is that wrong?"

"Wrong?" Grabinsky's face registered shock. "The altar is knocked over, and everything is destroyed. The paintings, the valuable carvings, everything *kaput!*" He covered his face with his hands and groaned. Then he looked up again and with more control said, "Only a real artist could estimate the damage. Damage in the millions!" His face became grim. "It will cost you plenty!"

"No, no!" Eric cried. "We had nothing to do with it!"

"Everyone claims to be innocent!" Grabinsky insisted. "No, it's not that simple. Come, have a look for yourself." With that he turned and walked rapidly toward the chapel.

The children looked at each other. Were they guilty after all? Several times they had inspected the altar and its paintings and carvings. Had one of them accidentally broken the support to the altar, causing it to crash later on? Filled with suspense, they entered the chapel and looked toward the altar.

There it stood in its usual place—nothing broken, nothing damaged!

"Yes, but..." Paul turned toward Grabinsky just as Tawny let out a painful yowl and the door slammed shut with a bang.

The five Bakers turned and froze. There stood two bearded men grinning at them. One of them had shoved the door shut, hitting Tawny. She did not seem to be hurt, but was barking angrily in the yard outside.

Before the children understood what was happening to them, the two men took advantage of their confusion, stepped forward, and each man grabbed two of them.

At the same moment Grabinsky grabbed Paul and held him in an iron grip. Paul reacted immediately and kicked the student's shins with his heel. Grabinsky tightened his grip until Paul could no longer breathe. Paul's face became even more red as Grabinsky growled, "Promise to be more friendly now?"

Prison Song

"Why are you doing this?" Anne stared at Grabinsky as she spoke. "You're a thief!"

"What crime have we committed?" Grabinsky replied. "My uncle does not value the paintings. Even so, he is receiving first-class reproductions, and we—well, we receive a little money. Therefore, everyone is better off than before."

"That's just criminal logic!" Anne snapped.

One of the men spoke up. "Why are you wasting time talking to these kids? We ought to be getting away."

"Not yet," answered Grabinsky. "The kids will not escape. We'll lock them up. Then you'll complete the paintings. My family loyalty demands that. The gallery of my ancestors must be complete, even if only as copies. Get that straight, Karl!"

The man named Karl let go of Katie and Anne a moment and stroked his long beard. "All right! Come, let's lock them up in the tunnel." With these words he again grabbed the girls.

Grabinsky gave Paul a shove. "Go, open the secret door!"

"How do you know...?" Paul started to ask.

"Ha—from you! I've been watching you from behind the altar! Now, hurry!"

Paul took a few steps toward the stone slab, then ran to the far side and called, "No!"

"Open that door immediately!" yelled Grabinsky.

Paul shook his head and glanced at the girls opposite him.

In an icy voice, the man Grabinsky had called Karl spoke. "Do you love your sisters?"

Paul nodded.

"Then do as you are told, or else..." With these words Karl tightened his grip on the girls' arms and they cried out in pain.

Paul gave up, climbed the stone slab, and released the secret mechanism.

"Max, you go first," Grabinsky ordered.

The third man nodded. He looked at the children, and it seemed to them that his brown eyes held kindness. He said in a soft voice, "You must be careful. It's slippery down there and..."

"They'll notice that soon enough!" Karl warned. "Hurry up!"

Max took a gas lamp from the first step and lit it. In its light the children found their way through the tunnel.

While Katie was watching the shadows dance across the moist walls, she thought maybe the men would not know the secret of the underground opening. But Max opened the door immediately, and her last hopes vanished. Quietly the group descended.

At the fork in the tunnel, Grabinsky said, "Come, Max, let them go ahead by themselves now. The tunnel is closed down up ahead, and there is no way of escape."

Turning to the children, he said gruffly, "You go farther on to the end. It's wider there."

To Karl, he continued, "You stay here and guard until someone comes to relieve you. It's narrow enough here so that no one can get by you. The lamp stays here. We will return in the darkness."

The children felt their way to the end of the tunnel.

Katie touched the floor and the walls. "Everything's wet. We'll catch our death of cold! What do we do now?"

No one answered.

After a few minutes, Rebecca sighed. "How long will they keep us here?"

"We can figure that out," said Katie. "Today is Wednesday. On Friday the paintings will be picked up. So we'll be here one or two days."

"We can't let them escape with those paintings!" declared Eric. "We must stop them."

"But how?" asked Rebecca hopelessly.

"The man who's guarding us will also want to make his getaway. If we keep an eye on him, we'll notice when he leaves," Paul said.

"That's a good idea!" Katie patted her brother on the shoulder.

"I have to sit down," Anne announced, taking off her raincoat and putting it on the ground. The others settled down on it with her. Katie put her coat around Anne's shoulders.

After about two hours, Paul stood up. "I just can't sit on the hard cold stones any more. I'm going over to the guard."

"Why are you going there?" Anne asked.

"To tell him we're freezing."

Paul's footsteps echoed down the tunnel. A minute later he was back.

"Well?" Katie inquired.

"They've changed off. Grabinsky is there now. He told me that everyone has to pay for the mistakes they make in life. He said we meddled and must now suffer for it. I told him that he will have to pay, too, and that though a prison cell may be more comfortable than this tunnel, he'll have several years there to enjoy it."

"Wow! What did he say to that?" Katie asked.

"He was mad, but I got away from him." Paul sat down again.

The five children were quiet for a long time.

Finally Eric broke the silence. "We're really pretty miserable Christians. I'm thinking of the three men in the fiery furnace. They could be happy in spite of their problems, because an angel was with them. Jesus promised us, too, 'I am with you always.' If we know that, why aren't we praising God?"

The others were silent.

Then Katie said slowly, "Yes, but maybe we should pray first. We learned Ephesians 5:19 and 20 in our Bible class. How does that go again? 'Speaking to one another in psalms and hymns...'"

"...and spiritual songs," added Rebecca.

Eric continued, "...singing and making melody in your heart..."

And now they all finished together, "...giving thanks always for all things to God the Father in the name of our Lord Jesus Christ."

"Come on, let's give thanks to God for our situation," urged Katie.

The children prayed together, thanking and praising God.

Rebecca started to sing, "Do not worry about your life, what you wear, for your heavenly Father cares for you," and the others joined in.

Two hours later, as the children sat quietly, sounds came to their ears. A beam of light came nearer.

It was the man the others had called Max. Under his arm he carried a foam mattress, a basket, and a lamp. He put the mattress down. "You must be tired. No one could sleep on these hard rocks, and surely you are hungry." He set the basket down on the floor. There were several tins of food in it, a can opener, and two candles.

"There," he said. "You must have a light so you can see what you are doing. I brought the candles from the altar in the chapel." His voice sounded friendly. "I hope this helps."

The children looked the cans over. They opened several and enjoyed the food. Then they sang more songs of praise, prayed together, and stretched out as well as they could on the mattress.

In the darkness, their guard had listened to all they said and sang. He went back to his spot with a sad face.

Way of Escape

After a few hours Eric awoke. He had slipped off the mattress onto the hard, cold rock floor. Without disturbing his sleeping brother and sisters, he stood up, stretched his aching body, and looked around. In the dim light of the candles he could just make out the caved-in part of the tunnel. He picked up a candle, went closer to the heap of rocks, and looked up at the ceiling.

Strange, he thought. *Everywhere else the tunnel is carefully carved out. Only at this one place has it caved in, even though the rocks here don't seem to be any more crumbly than anywhere else. I wonder what happened.*

He returned, sat down on an empty corner of the mattress, and stared thoughtfully into a flickering candle flame. He remembered reading a book in which children explore some underground tunnels. Suddenly he sat up with a jerk. In that book the children tested the level of oxygen in the air with a candle! If the flame became smaller or even went out, it meant danger. He looked over at the candle, which flickered lightly. Eric held his breath and stared at the light without moving.

That little flicker is possibly only in a draft, he thought. *That's why the air here is fresh.* Slowly he got to his feet, took the candle, climbed up on the six-foot high pile of rubble, and examined the rocks. A draft could be coming in only where the rock ceiling and the rubble met. He set the candle down on the floor in a number of places. At one spot the flame bent over sideways. Eric reached up with his hand to feel between the rocks. At one place there was a weak draft. Full of excitement he removed some of the rocks and pushed them over to the side.

Suddenly a rock rolled down the heap and rumbled down onto the tunnel floor. Eric grabbed the candle and bounded back to the mattress. He put his head down and listened intently. Footsteps were approaching. What should he do? The cold around him gave him an idea. He jumped up, stretched and yawned, and began doing jumping jacks, slapping his arms vigorously against his body.

Grabinsky called out to him, "Hey, what was the crashing sound?"

"I'm doing calisthenics. Aren't you cold?" Eric replied.

"That's none of your business!" With these words Grabinsky turned and went back down the passage.

Eric thought, *Now or never!* and carefully he sneaked after the art student. In the light of the gas lamp he watched Grabinsky sit down on a lawn chair at the narrowest point in the tunnel.

There's no chance of escaping there, thought Eric unhappily. Disappointed, he made his way back. Once more he carefully climbed up on the rubble and determined that at the place where he had removed the rock there was definitely a draft. Reluctantly he climbed down and sat on the mattress. There was no point in taking more rocks away if even the softest of footsteps echoed down the tunnel. Their guard would be sure to hear. Slowly fatigue took over, and Eric fell back asleep.

About six o'clock Paul woke and roused Eric, who immediately recounted his discovery.

"If only we could escape and reach the police before it's too late," Paul said. "Hey, I know what we should do! When the girls wake up, we'll eat, then we'll sing songs for a long time. Meanwhile, one of us will try to move some rocks."

A half hour later the girls awoke. Quietly the boys shared their plan. The girls agreed enthusiastically.

"I have another idea," Anne added. "The tunnel makes a slight bend here. If we go a little farther in toward the entrance, the candle up on the heap can no longer be seen. I mean, just in case one of the men pays us a visit."

The others thought that was a good idea, so they took the mattress and the cans and carried them some fifty feet closer to the fork of the passage. Paul took the candle and climbed up on the rubble heap.

"What are we going to sing?" Anne asked the other children.

"Why?" Katie asked.

"Well, usually we sing Christian songs, but now we're singing just to cover up sounds. So I don't think we should sing songs of praise without thinking about God."

"You're right!" agreed Rebecca. "Let's sing folk songs."

As the songs echoed from the tunnel, Paul dug

the rocks out of the sand and mud as quickly as he could and carefully laid them aside. It was hard work, and he made very slow progress.

After a while Eric relieved him.

When Paul returned to the others, Katie asked him, "Well, how does it look?"

"Not too good! A huge rock is blocking the opening. We'll never move it!"

"Can't you work your way around it, to one side of it?" Anne asked.

"Well, yes, we'll have to, but then all our work so far has been for nothing."

Suddenly a light appeared in the distance. Rebecca listened to the footsteps and whispered, "I think it's the one they call Max. Quickly! Go tell Eric."

Max appeared out of the darkness and asked how they were.

"How long will we have to be imprisoned here?" Anne inquired.

"Probably another day!" Max answered apologetically. "Early tomorrow the paintings will be picked up. Add to that a bit of lead time, and you'll be free by lunch."

"Another day!" groaned Rebecca.

"I'm really sorry, but nothing can be changed now," Max answered, looking helpless.

"I'd like to ask you something." Katie gave him a serious look. "You are a nice, friendly person. How did you become a criminal?"

Max took a deep breath and began. "I was always an honest man. I have never been in trouble with the law. And this all started out so harmlessly. Grabinsky told us that his uncle, Baron von Zerbach, had often expressed the wish to move the paintings of his ancestors into his own castle, but decided not to do it, because these people had lived here. He also explained that his uncle had asked about having the paintings copied. He promised Karl and me a very large sum of money to complete the job. He even offered us a sizable advance. Such a good offer does not come along every day, so we accepted the advance payment. Karl was able to set up a new studio with it, and I made a trip to Italy to study art."

"When we arrived here, I thought it was strange that we had to work in a secret place. Grabinsky gave us many reasons for that. He told us he wanted to surprise his uncle for his fiftieth birthday. He said that the baron often visited the castle quite unexpectedly. We were hidden so he wouldn't notice us."

"When did you realize that you were being tricked?" asked Eric.

"Not long ago. Grabinsky wanted to go out on business. After he'd already left, Karl remembered something he wanted and ran after him. At the door he overheard a telephone conversation by Grabinsky. It was obvious that the original paintings were to be sold abroad.

"We were both shocked and confronted him with the information. He admitted the truth, but put pressure on us by demanding his money back. That's why we had to continue and have become his accomplices. Because of you there has been a change. The story will come out. Even if no one knows our names, we still must live in constant fear of being found out."

He sighed and hung his head. "We only wanted to earn a lot of money, and instead we have become criminals. We will be fugitives and may never even get the money. But we came to this conclusion too late."

The children felt sorry for him. They realized that he had been tricked into forging the paintings.

After some time Max spoke again. "I was close to you yesterday and heard your songs and your prayers. Do you think God could help me?"

The children nodded silently.

"But how?" Max looked at them earnestly.

"You will have to take the punishment for what you did," answered Anne. "But if you ask Jesus to forgive you, He will do that, and God will not punish you further."

"I am not a godless man," Max replied. "I even attend church once in a while, but I realize now that there is more to really believing. I would not have buckled under so badly and..." He choked up.

And?" asked Paul.

"And I will do so again."

"Do so again?"

"Yes. I should let you go so you could call the police, but I don't have the inner strength to do that." He turned and walked slowly away, leaving the children behind.

Paul broke the silence. "I'm going back to work. Sing a few more folk songs."

Feverishly he scratched the soft sand from the rocks. The rough rock rubbed the skin from his fingers, but he paid no attention to it. He dislodged a large stone and put his hand up to feel the opening. His fingers found another rock. When he tried to move it, the rock slipped through his fingers and rolled forward into the space beyond. Paul barely stifled a cheer. He hurried back to the others to tell them the news.

After that the girls sang even more exuberantly.

Both boys returned to the heap and dug as if in a race. Soon the opening was large enough that Eric could squeeze through it. Paul handed him the candle and then also wiggled through. Full of excitement they crept along the passage on the other side. It went downhill. To the left another tunnel seemed to open up. The boys entered it, but after about six feet they were stopped by a huge wooden door.

Eric felt around. "Solid oak! I wonder if it opens?"

The two boys put their shoulders to it, but couldn't budge it.

"No doorknob in sight. Probably bolted from the inside," Paul guessed. "Come on! Let's continue in the first tunnel."

After about thirty feet Eric stopped and pointed ahead excitedly. A faint beam of light in the distance! The boys hurried on. After a few more steps they stopped again.

"What's that strange noise?" Paul looked at his brother. "It's a rushing sound."

Eric peered at the many drops of water in the ceiling above. "Is it the brook?"

"That's possible," Paul said. "Let's go."

The light showed that they were near the end of the tunnel. Ahead the boys stood before a door, a stone slab about three feet wide and five feet high. One corner was badly weathered, and the light was coming in through this fist-sized opening.

Paul bent down and peered out. "We're right under the brook! I can see the waterfall!"

"Can you enlarge the hole?" Eric asked.

"I'll try! The rock has become a little porous in all this moisture, and it's crumbling off in layers." Paul broke off a piece as he was talking.

"Should I try?" Eric offered.

"We can take turns. It's not hard."

Slowly the hole grew larger as Paul continued to break off the crumbling rock around the door opening.

"That's it! No more of it will break away," he said after some time.

"Would my head fit through?" Eric asked.

Paul shrugged his shoulders. "Try it!"

Eric climbed up on his brother's shoulders and tried. "My head goes through, but not my body."

"Put your arms through first!"

"No, it still doesn't work! It's just too small."

When Eric was back on the floor, he rubbed his arms. "Those edges are sharp."

"This is rough!" groaned Paul. "We can see freedom, but we can't get out. Come on, we have to go back."

The girls were anxiously awaiting the boys.

"Hurry, tell us what's going on?" Katie begged.

The boys quickly told their story.

"A locked wooden door," Katie said. "We'll have to investigate that as soon as we are free again."

"Yes, when we're free again!" Anne said.

Slowly the candles burned down. Rebecca put one out, saying, "We'll save this one. Maybe we'll need it."

While the two boys slept on the mattress, the girls passed their time by reciting Bible verses and reviewing Latin and German grammar and other things they had learned at school. Still the hours passed much too slowly.

Missing!

That morning, in the midst of heavy rain, the Martin boys came to the castle as promised. No one answered the door.

"That's strange!" said Andreas. "No one here! Could they be in the palace?"

Suddenly they heard a friendly bark.

"It's Tawny!" Simon said. When she came to him, he stroked her head. "She's very wet."

"Maybe they're all out walking, and Tawny just came back ahead of them," Markus suggested.

The three boys went to the castle gate and waited for some time. No one came.

"Something is wrong here!" Markus declared. "They wouldn't go away and leave the dog out in the rain."

The boys went back to the door of the apartment. Markus looked around the corner. "There's an open window here."

"Hello!" he shouted, but no one answered. "I'm climbing in through the window and opening the door," he announced to his brothers.

When the three boys stood inside, Andreas said,

"Look, here's where their raincoats were hanging. Their rubber boots are gone too. Something has happened!"

Andreas turned to Markus with a laugh. "You seem to think that as the son of a police inspector you have to see something strange in every situation."

"Do you have a better idea?"

"Well, it's possible that they left the dog at home because of the rain, and he opened the door and jumped out!"

"Oh, and do you think that a dog could open a French window that was locked?" Markus asked with a grin.

"Certainly not, but maybe it wasn't locked."

"All right. Let's give it a try!"

Andreas pulled the window closed but did not bolt it. The boys ran outside, leaving the dog in the apartment. At the window they called, "Tawny. Come, Tawny!"

The dog pushed her nose against the window, and it opened. She jumped out with one huge leap to join the boys. Andreas looked at his brother in triumph.

"All right," mumbled Markus. "I give up!"

The three boys took the dog back into the apartment and locked the door before leaving. In the evening, at six and again at eight, Markus called the apartment, but no one answered. When two hours later there was still no answer, the boys went to their father.

"You're telling quite a story!" he said. "Come, let's have a look."

When the car drew near, its headlights shone on the castle walls and flashed across the window at the art student's quarters. Grabinsky sprang up and went over to the drapes. His mind was working feverishly when the doorbell rang. He opened the door and in a soft, polite voice asked what he could do for Herr Martin.

"The children?" Grabinsky said. "Yes, I talked to them at noon. I asked them where they were off to in this awful weather, and they said they were hiking to the bears' den. When I inquired where that was, they said about ten kilometers away. But they were going to be back by tonight."

Inspector Martin shook his head. "This is a very rocky area. They would need four hours just to get there. What should we do?"

"I think I'd just wait," answered Grabinsky calmly. "There are five of them, so nothing could happen to all of them at the same time. If they're not back tomorrow morning, I'll call the police."

"That's not necessary. They're already here!" Inspector Martin said.

"What?" Grabinsky was startled. "Where?"

"Right here! I'm Inspector Martin."

Grabinsky took a deep breath. "Yes, of course. I met your wife Good, so you'll look after them, and I'll find out tomorrow what happened. So long then. Goodnight!"

Slowly the police inspector drove away. "There's something strange here," he said.

"Why?" Markus looked at his father.

"An honest man is surprised or curious if the police show up. This Grabinsky was startled, as if he had a bad conscience. I'm going to keep an eye on him."

"And what do we do now?"

"We'll send out a search order, so someone will begin to look for the American children right away. I'll take some men with dogs and search also."

"May we come?" Simon asked.

"No, no. Don't be insulted, but this is work for men!"

Grabinsky watched the car leave. *I'd better not tell Karl and Max about this,* he thought. *It would only make them nervous. Besides, tomorrow morning we'll be gone forever!*

Breakthrough

All day the children had taken turns sleeping, and now at two in the morning they were wide awake. Eric opened a tin of pineapple. Thoughtfully he inspected the sharp can opener and the spoon with which he was eating.

"What are you thinking about?" Katie asked.

Eric looked up. "The hole at the end of the tunnel. Maybe I could enlarge it with the help of these."

"Would that work?"

"I'll give it a try!" Eric climbed up the rubble heap and slithered through the opening to the other side. Then he clambered over to the end of the tunnel as quickly as he could. With the pointed end of the can opener he tore at the stone and then scratched away with the spoon. After nearly an hour he stopped to rest and examined his work. The opening had become somewhat bigger, but would there be time enough to make it large enough to get through? *We'll just wait and see*, he thought and scratched away again.

Around eight in the morning both Paul and Eric were still at work trying to enlarge the opening. The girls sat quietly on the mattress, waiting.

Meanwhile a van had arrived at the castle to pick up the paintings. Grabinsky found his way through the secret tunnel once again. He wanted the children to realize as late as possible that they were no longer being guarded. In a few hours he and his companions would be over the hills and far away.

When Grabinsky reached the spot where the girls were, he was startled. "Where are your brothers?" he demanded.

"Oh, they just had to go off and do something private," answered Rebecca.

"Okay. Unfortunately I must tell you that there have been some delays. You'll have to stay here another day. I'm sorry! But I see that you still have enough food."

He was about to leave them, when once more he asked suspiciously, "What's keeping the boys?"

"Oh, they'll be right here," stammered Rebecca.

"Call them!"

"Paul! Eric!" Anne shouted. "Come here at once! Herr Grabinsky would like to see you."

When there was no reply, the art student muttered, "Something's wrong!"

"Should I run and find out?" Anne jumped to her feet.

"No, you stay here!" yelled Grabinsky. But Anne ran a few yards toward the rubble heap and called loudly, "Hurry, Paul! Eric, hurry! Herr Grabinsky is here!"

The art student gave an angry yell, and shoved Katie and Rebecca ahead of him to the rubble. He looked up, and when he saw the opening, which was much too small for his body, he howled with

128

rage. "You'll pay for this!" he yelled. "Don't you dare leave this place! I won't be responsible for what might happen!"

With these words he stumbled off, cursing.

When the two boys heard that Grabinsky was looking for them, they tried the seemingly impossible.

"Hurry!" called Paul. "Get up on my shoulders and try to squeeze through the hole!"

Eric got stuck at the shoulders. "I can't," he complained.

"Stretch your arms high!" commanded Paul.

Eric put his arms and head through the opening. Paul grabbed his legs and pushed forcefully.

"Ouch!" cried Eric.

"Blow out all your breath!" Paul yelled. "And hold your legs real stiff." He took a step back, shouted, "Run fast to the police!" and rammed his chest against Eric's feet. Pow! Eric's legs disappeared through the opening. From outside came a short gurgling cry, and Eric disappeared behind the falling wall of water. Then all was still again.

Paul took a deep breath, closed his eyes and prayed, "Lord, please let him get to the police station on time." Then he ran back to the girls. They quickly reported everything to him.

"What? And you're still here?" he cried out.

"Well, what are we supposed to do?"

"Don't you understand? Grabinsky must be with the others, so no one is guarding us. Come on, we're free! And we're leaving!"

"Going where?" Anne asked.

"To the mill, of course!" Paul picked up the candle and started off running. The girls stumbled after him.

Meanwhile Grabinsky ran across the courtyard.

129

"How near finished are you?" he asked Karl.

"Two more paintings to load!"

"Hurry!" Grabinsky shouted.

"Why?"

"Don't ask! Just move!"

He ran into his house, grabbed his luggage, and dragged it out. He stowed it in the trunk, then ran up the stairs to pick up the suitcases of his companions. Just when the last painting had been brought down from the secret workshop, Grabinsky arrived with the last suitcase.

"Quick! Let's go!" he called to the driver. The van left. Grabinsky, Karl, and Max jumped into the station wagon.

"Once we've left the village, we're safe," said Grabinsky as he stepped on the gas.

Meanwhile the four children had reached the mill. Anne looked out of the window toward the castle road. "I wonder if they've left already?"

"I hope not!" Katie exclaimed.

"I wonder if Eric managed to reach the police," Paul said.

Anne reported, "Someone's closing car doors! If only we could stop them."

Paul stared at Anne. "Stop a speeding car?"

"I know!" Katie opened the window and climbed out. "Come on!"

"Where to?" Paul asked.

"Did you see the pile of logs beside the road? We'll roll them into the road!" The children left the mill and ran after Katie. With a combined effort they pulled up the small stakes that held the logs in place. This loosened the logs, which rolled out onto the road. In a matter of seconds the road was blocked.

"Listen, they're coming!" yelled Paul. "Let's hide

behind the mill. If they chase us, we'll each run in a different direction."

The two vehicles braked. The men scrambled out and began rolling, pushing, and pulling the logs to clear the road.

The children watched from the corner of the mill.

"If only the police come soon!" Rebecca whispered.

Eric, out of breath, arrived at the police station. After only a few sentences the men understood. Quickly one went to the radio and called officers in patrol cars.

Inspector Martin was standing near his police car, together with his men, feeling rather hopeless. A few minutes ago they had called off the search for the children. Suddenly their radio crackled with a message. The men jumped into their cars and raced with screaming sirens toward the village.

Meanwhile the police in the patrol car had been observing the men on the road near the castle. Inspector Martin, racing along at breakneck speed, was giving orders. Between the first two houses four patrol cars formed a barricade across the road. When the inspector reached the outskirts of the village, he ordered all sirens shut off.

The art thieves had cleared their lane of logs, climbed back into the vehicles, and started off again. When they approached the village, their blood ran cold! Behind them was Inspector Martin's siren; ahead of them, patrol cars blocking the street! Police, with guns drawn, approached the two cars. Before the men could do anything, the police had pulled them from the vehicles, frisked them for weapons, and snapped on handcuffs.

A minute later there was a screech of brakes and Inspector Martin jumped from his car. When he saw that his radioed instructions had been followed, he said, "Well done, men! That was teamwork! Take them to the station. I'll be there soon, but first I must locate the children."

"One of them is here," called an officer, pointing to Eric. He was wet and muddy and stood leaning against the wall. Inspector Martin came over to him and put a hand on his shoulder, saying, "You did well! Come, we'll drive out to find the others."

The four were standing at the roadside close to the castle and, with great relief, waved at the police car. Quickly they piled in. When they were back on the grounds of the castle, tears came to the eyes of the girls. Inspector Martin put his arm around Rebecca, saying, "It was tough on all of you, but you really were brave. I must go back to the station, but tonight we'll pick you up and we'll go out for pizza!"

That evening the five Bakers sat with the Martins in the pizza place, eating and chattering away. The restaurant had quickly filled up with curious people. It was an important event for these villagers. They never before had seen so many policemen and patrol cars in one spot.

After the meal Inspector Martin went for his guitar. They sang until late in the night. All who heard were impressed, and many joined in the songs about Jesus.

Unexpected Guests

Early the next morning the doorbell rang at the Baker apartment. Still sleepy, Rebecca found her way to the door and opened the tiny window to peek out. There she saw Baron von Zerbach and his wife. When she opened the door, they greeted her with a cheerful "Good morning."

Spontaneously the baron gave her a hug and said, "I'm sorry that you have had to suffer so much at the hands of my nephew. Inspector Martin called me last night and told me everything."

"Well," said Rebecca graciously, "it was scary, but we made it."

When she realized that they were still standing in the doorway, she said, "Oh, I'm not being very polite! Please come in. We just woke up and haven't had breakfast yet. Won't you join us?"

"Oh, thank you! That sounds good, because we have driven all night and have had no chance to eat yet," the baron replied.

Soon breakfast was ready, and immediately after the prayer the baron continued his story. "Inspector Martin told me all about your adventure." He shook his head. "It could have had a tragic ending."

Paul shrugged his shoulders. "Not really for us. It would have been hard if we had to stay in the tunnel any more days, but it could have meant an unhappy ending for the paintings too."

"Oh, yes," agreed the baron. "Who knows whether we ever would have seen them again if they had disappeared abroad. You saved something very valuable. We are so grateful!"

"You said the paintings are valuable," Katie replied. "Maybe there are other valuable things still waiting for us." Katie's face took on a wistful look. "Last year you told us about a second treasure, which has never been found, and which belonged to the nobles. Maybe now we have a lead." Katie quietly continued her breakfast.

"Look at her! I'm holding my breath with excitement," said the baron, "and she eats peacefully!"

"Is it in connection with the secret tunnels you discovered?" asked the baroness.

Paul entered the conversation. "I think I'd better explain. Beyond the rubble heap, we found a heavy oak door closing off the passage. Unfortunately it was locked, apparently from the inside."

"In which direction did the tunnel run?" the baron inquired.

Eric moved a couple of plates and cups and began to explain. "Well, here, this is the castle, and there is the mill. The passage runs from the chapel, probably under the western tower, through to the outer tower. From there to about here is the fork. The tunnel going straight ahead leads to the mill; the one to the left, to the rubble heap." Eric tapped the table. "The door is about here. It's possible that the tunnel comes back to the castle again."*

"More precisely, to the front part of the castle," added Paul, "but where could it end? There's no basement under that part of the castle."

The baron thought about this, his eyes staring at a picture on the wall opposite him. Suddenly he said, "Maybe it is a lead after all. I just thought of something from years ago. Let's see." He tapped the cup that represented the round tower in the inner castle. "The wall that leads from this point separates the front part from the main part of the castle. And it runs directly east to west."

"Why do all these towers open up to the inside?" asked Eric.

"That is quite easy to explain," answered the baron. "Suppose the castle were invaded. The enemy would have no opportunity to establish a hold in these towers, because they open to the inside and could be fired upon from other parts of the castle. That was the only reason. Now, let's continue. You told me that the tunnel leads through the western tower. That leaves the northern tower."

Katie took a deep breath and tried to interrupt, but the baron held up his hand. "Just a moment! The explanation is coming to me now! Many years ago a teacher in the town pieced together a history of the castle."

"We met this teacher last summer," Rebecca said.

---

*See map: The secret tunnel goes from the chapel (#14) under the western tower (#15) through to the outer tower (#9), to the fork (#2), to the waterfall (#5). Halfway between #2 and #5 is the rubble heap. A little beyond that, near #3, is the secret oak door.

Baron von Zerbach nodded at the children. "This teacher made a thorough search of the castle and concluded that underneath both the round towers, the western and the northern, there must be cellars. He had dug down through the clay and in both places found a big vault. Because no one would build such a vault with a good reason, he thought there were cellars below. But no one could figure out a reason for it, so this discovery was forgotten. Now you have proved that there is a basement under the western tower, because you went through the tower and saw the vault above. If the northern tower is built in the same way, the tunnel could lead there."

"Great!" Katie exclaimed.

"There should be some way, then, of getting to it from the castle," Paul suggested.

The baron nodded. "You are right!"

"So far it's still all a theory," the baroness said. "You must try to prove your theory."

"Let's go!" Eric jumped up.

"Take it easy!" Anne said. "First we have our prayer, then we clean up, and then we go."

After a half hour, six persons were finding their way through the tunnel.

The baron seemed deeply moved. "For many decades I have owned this castle, but I never knew these secret tunnels."

Using two spades they had brought, the boys quickly enlarged the hole above the rubble heap. Soon they all were standing before the wooden door. The baron put his weight against it. Nothing moved.

Eric picked up a rock and knocked against the wood.

"It sounds thick," said Katie.

Then Eric pounded both the right and the left of the door. But the wall seemed solid everywhere.

"May I try it up here?" the baron asked. He took the piece of rock and tapped the upper section of the wall. At one place the sound was more hollow. The children looked at the wall expectantly. After a few more taps, cracks appeared. Suddenly a small square piece fell out, revealing an opening.

"Come, Paul, up on my shoulders and have a look."

"Wipe your feet," warned Eric. "You're stepping on royal flesh and blood!"

The baron gave him a playful jab in the ribs. Paul climbed up on the baron's strong shoulders.

"Do you see anything?" the baron asked.

"Yes," shouted Paul. "A rope!"

"Be careful," cautioned the baron. "It may be rotten. Shine the light in."

"The hole is about three feet deep," Paul said. "Behind it is a narrow room."

"Where does the rope lead to?"

"Down."

"The rope may have been used to lift a wooden bolt. Pull on it very gently."

Paul gave one small tug and ended up with a short length of rope in his hands.

"We could have known that would happen," the baron said. "Shine the light in once more and then describe the place in detail."

"It's narrow," Paul said.

"It could be a hall," suggested Anne.

"Maybe," agreed Paul. "But I can tell you only what I see. If it continues to the left, then it probably is a hall, but I can't tell for sure."

"What do we do now?" Rebecca asked.

"Let's knock the door down," Katie suggested.

Baron von Zerbach looked at her. "You'd really like to find out what lies beyond the door, wouldn't you?"

"We all would!" Katie replied.

"Yes, but I have a deep respect for the work of my ancestors, and I do not like to destroy anything they built."

"I have an idea!" Eric exclaimed. "Last year when we found the secret well tunnel, we used a mirror. With a hand-held mirror and a flashlight we could have a look at the wooden bolt from the top and then maybe use some clothesline to lift the bolt."

"We'd have to buy some," Katie said, "or borrow some from the Martins. I bet that Andreas, Markus and Simon would love to be a part of our adventure."

"Good idea! I'll go with you," Rebecca offered.

"We'll stay in the tunnel," suggested the baron, "and study the whole situation more closely."

The two girls hurried off. The others stayed near the door.

"I'd like to know how, in the olden days, they made the stone doors so they would move," Paul said.

"The principle involved is simple. Do you see those two cemented-in holes?" the baron asked. "The door was made so that on each side of it there was a long pivot sticking out."

"Oh, the door would rotate in those holes then," Paul said.

"Yes. There was then an opening of about one meter width and maybe 60 centimeters high. Earlier the bottom half of it was the rock," explained the baron. "If the fleeing owners were discovered, and they did manage to close the door in time, the small opening was quite easy to defend. One must not

138

forget either that the waterfall also forms a natural barrier."

"Could the door be opened from the outside?" Eric asked.

"No, because, as you see here, the stone door is fitted very precisely into the frame. You can hardly see a crack. Secondly, it was necessary only to put a boulder on the inside between the lower part of the door and the back wall in order to lock it securely. Nobody could move it then."

"Not bad!" Paul exclaimed.

"Oh, our ancestors were not stupid!" the baron replied. "Come, let's go to the blocked section of the tunnel."

Paul, Eric and Anne followed Baron von Zerbach. At one point, he stopped abruptly and shone his light on a small hole in the ceiling.

"A vent," he said. "The tunnel had to have some fresh air. Air could come in through these vents."

Anne raised her hand. "I don't feel any breeze."

"I would imagine that, over the centuries, the ·root of a tree or some dirt has closed the vent."

"How could such a vent be chiseled out? It's too small for a person to fit into it," Paul asked.

"It was not easy, but it was necessary. First a wider shaft was made, then it was lined with bricks to become the smaller vent. The upper opening was camouflaged with large rocks and brush. I would think a tunnel like this one would have three or four such vents."

The group continued toward the rubble pile.

"Here I am somewhat puzzled." Baron von Zerbach flashed his light all around. "There are several possibilities to explain what happened here, since a natural caving in of the rock walls is not possible. Maybe it was a cleverly set trap, such

140

as you found last year."

"And it sprang shut?" Eric suggested.

"That we will never know!" the baron replied. "The tunnel also could have been damaged by explosives meant to block the tunnel leading to the castle."

After they had explored the tunnels a while longer, they heard voices in the distance. Katie, Rebecca, and the three Martin boys appeared.

Back again at the wooden door, the baron took Markus up on his shoulders. The boy took the flashlight and a mirror so that he could see the inside of the room.

"Yes, I can see everything," he exclaimed. "Please hand me the clothesline."

Markus took the rope, made a loop, and carefully let it down. Everyone watched him in suspense. Again and again he tried to slide a loop around the wooden bolt. At last he ordered, "Pull!"

The boys tugged carefully on the rope.

"Harder!" urged the baron.

All the children pulled.

"I'll count to three, and on three you really tug. One, two, three."

Suddenly the rope went slack, and all the children tumbled onto the rocky floor.

Andreas jumped up immediately and pushed at the door. It moved just a bit.

"It's open!" he cried. "Come, give me a hand."

Together they all pushed the door open. It creaked in protest.

The baron looked at the children. "Now for the real surprise! Come!"

After a few yards the tunnel ahead took a slight bend to the right and led upward. Here and there rough steps were hewn into the floor.

The baron stopped. "If I'm not mistaken, we are already underneath the castle."

The way was very steep, almost like a stairway.

"Look!" Paul stopped and pointed upward. "Another vent. I can really feel the draft here."

"Hmm," said the baron. "I think this passage must end in the north wall. If that is true, we are very near our destination."

The group moved on, filled with anticipation.

"The tunnel ends up there," Paul called. He hurried ahead. "A spiral staircase leads upward."

"It's really narrow!" exclaimed Eric.

"It had to be, so it could be defended easily," Paul said.

"You are well informed," praised the baron.

Paul and Andreas hurried ahead and called back, "Here's another tunnel."

The spiral staircase ended on a small platform. A wooden door shut off the way beyond. Toward the left another tunnel branched off, but after about thirty feet ended at the wall.

The children looked at the baron.

He did not seem at all disappointed. "My theory stands. The wooden door leads to the basement below the northern tower of the main building and this wall is...well, who can guess?"

Simon's face lit up. "The tunnel from the well?"

"Right! The same tunnel in which you children found the skeleton in your previous adventure. The passage did make a bend after three meters, right? That's the place we're at now, I think. Look at the wall. Later it becomes part of the tunnel."*

---

*See map: This tunnel leads from #3 to the northern tower (#16) and from there to the well (#17).

"And what will we find in the tower cellar?" Simon asked.

"We shall see. If the castle has one more secret, then it certainly is there."

With hearts pounding the children returned to the door. The boys pushed hard. The wood did not seem as thick, because the door heaved and groaned under the pressure.

"I wish we had a key," Rebecca said.

"It wouldn't do any good, because the whole lock is rusty," said Paul. "But if we all push at the same time, maybe it will open."

The baron agreed. "I know of no other way. Okay— one, two, three..."

The wood groaned slightly, then the door opened with a creak. The children entered a high-ceilinged cellar, which was covered with a huge criss-crossed vault. The baron's flashlight revealed three huge chests of wood, standing side by side on the wet floor. None of the children moved to touch them.

Slowly the baron approached and grasped the lid of the middle chest. Slowly he opened it. His eyes fell on a leather pouch. He reached into the bag. When he took it out and opened it, there were large gold pieces shimmering in his hand.

"The treasure! The treasure!" Eric cried.

All the children joined in the cheer.

After they had calmed down, the baron gave each child a gold piece. "As a souvenir of this moment! It is something of a down payment. The real reward will come later."

In a mood of celebration the children started on their way back. After a few yards Rebecca stopped. "Something has been cemented in here," she said as she shined her light on the wall.

The baron smiled. "Do you know where this door leads to?"

The children thought hard, but could not guess.

"It must lead to the secret cellar you discovered a year ago."

"Right!" agreed Eric. "We saw several cemented spots. If Professor Crippen had broken through this wall, he could have found the treasure—unless he would have fallen into some other trap."*

Back in the castle yard Eric spoke for all of them. "This was a real adventure!"

*See map: This tunnel goes from #3 to the northern tower (#16). The short well tunnel goes from #16 to #17. At #17 it was joined to the castle wall. Originally it extended to #18. The conversation between the baron and the children took place at #24. The story about the secret cellar and the skeleton near the well is told in *The Secret Treasure*.

Farewell to the Castle

The next day was Sunday, but it was no day of
rest. After the church service, in which the
children gave thanks to God for protection, there
was a lunch in the Knights' Hall. The baron and his
wife had invited the Bakers and the Martins. It was a
great celebration. Candles were burning on the
tables, and a fire crackled in the huge fireplace.
After a prayer and song everyone enjoyed the good
food, delivered by a local restaurant. Between two
courses the baron made a speech and announced
that at the insistence of the news media a press
conference had been scheduled for that afternoon.

At the conference the children revealed all the
details of their adventure. It took nearly three
hours.

"I've never been photographed so much in my
life!" Anne sighed.

The children had another happy week of
vacation, in which they revisited many places in the
castle. Naturally they all insisted on finding the
secret painting workshop. They found the entrance

145

under a slanting roof, cleverly hidden by a second wooden wall.*

The original paintings from the Knights' Hall were placed in a museum. The copies stayed at the castle after an agreement was reached with Grabinsky.

As the Baker children were about to return to their parents, Baron von Zerbach had one more surprise for them.

"When I gave you each a gold coin, I said it was only a down payment. Your real reward for finding the treasure is still to come. My family owns a castle in Scotland. During your next school break, I will treat you to a vacation at our Scottish castle—all expenses paid!"

"Hurray! Next year in Scotland!" Katie cried.

A few weeks later the children received a letter from prison.

"It's from Max," Anne announced. "He says that he now believes in Jesus Christ and knows that Jesus is always with those who love Him. He says here, 'Your example of faith helped.'"

"That's great!" Rebecca exclaimed.

"Let's thank the Lord for that, and let's pray for Karl and Herr Grabinsky."

the end

---

*See map: Midway between #26 and #22 is the secret entrance to the painting workshop. The workshop is #22.